BOOK TWO OF THE GUARDIANS

GUARDIANS
OF THE
SKY

S.L. WILSON

AMBER
PUBLISHING

Cover design, interior book design,
and eBook design
by Blue Harvest Creative
www.blueharvestcreative.com

GUARDIANS OF THE SKY

Published by
Amber Publishing

ISBN-13: 978-1523258307
ISBN-10: 1523258306

Visit the author at:

Websites: *www.shelleywilsonauthor.co.uk* and *www.bhcauthors.com*
Facebook: *www.facebook.com/FantasyAuthorSLWilson*
Twitter: *www.twitter.com/ShelleyWilson72*
Instagram: *www.instagram.com/authorslwilson*

Visit the author's website
by scanning the QR code.

Also By
S.L. Wilson

Guardians of the Dead
Book 1 of The Guardians

Guardians of the Lost Lands
Book 3 of The Guardians
Releases December 2016

For mum and dad.
You always believed.

To Rebekah
with love

Shelley Wilson :)

x

GUARDIANS
OF THE
SKY

CHAPTER I

Amber observed the comings and goings at the castle from her secluded spot in the forest. Wrapped in a warm cloak and concealed beneath her hood, she melted into the greenery of her surroundings. Connor had climbed the nearest sweet chestnut tree in the hope of getting a better look at Nikita's defences. Since arriving in the faerie realm, his half-fae heritage had evolved, and Amber watched in mild amusement, as he scaled the tree with the ease of any fae warrior. From her lower hiding place, Amber could only make out the golden gate and the two menacing minotaurs on guard.

It seemed like only a few days ago that she'd thought minotaurs didn't exist, except in Greek mythology. The shocking discovery that witches, demons, and necromancers were parading around her hometown had turned her stomach. The added revelation that she was also of supernatural origin further fuelled her discord.

Descended from oracles, Amber's ancient powers had been thrust upon her without the aid of a tutorial, mentor, or Google map. She was in the throes of learning on the job.

Until recently, she and Connor had been a couple of normal teenagers, living their mundane lives in the human world. The possibility of fighting demons and travelling across realms didn't exist;

until a supernatural guardian kidnapped her best friend, Tom. With help from India, Connor's Wiccan aunt, they had managed to rescue Tom from the clutches of an evil General. In the process, she discovered that her mother was being held captive in the same place, alongside Alia, a faerie queen, and Prince Redka.

When they had escaped, and the faerie portal spat them out here in Avaveil, Amber believed that it would be a temporary visit. As it turned out, Avaveil was under threat from Alia's sister and their plans changed as quickly as the weather. Agreeing to help Queen Alia reclaim her lands meant that going home would have to wait a while.

Her mother, who until a fortnight ago had been absent from her life for ten years, was trying to teach her the ways of witchcraft. As a skilled witch and past coven leader, Myanna was an outstanding tutor, however it quickly became apparent that spells and Amber didn't mix. So far she had burnt down a faerie warrior's dwelling, blown a rock sky high, and temporarily turned Tom's hair green.

PULLED FROM her thoughts, she watched Connor drop lightly from the tree to land beside her.

She leaned in close. 'Anything?'

'She's got minotaurs surrounding the perimeter and about fifty of them in the inner circle, but that's all I could see.' He dusted a stray leaf from his jacket.

'Ah, but she could have an army of dwarves milling around the grand ballroom.' Amber raised her eyebrows and wiggled them until Connor smiled at her.

'How can you joke at a time like this? We've agreed to postpone finding our way back to the human world, help a fae queen overthrow her evil sister, *and* live in the woods with insects as big as a dog!' He flung his arms wide to demonstrate the exaggerated size of the woodland critters.

Amber chuckled softly. 'I have to joke. Otherwise I'll go crazy and blow up a few more rocks.'

'It's a pity you can't just blow up the castle and save us all the work.' Connor wiggled his eyebrows this time, and she playfully slapped him on the arm.

'Not sure Alia would approve of my blowing up her home. Besides, if we can't find our way back to Hills Heath we might be living in there soon.' She inclined her head in the direction of the imposing castle. The buttery cream colour of the stone glistened in the fading light of the sun. Two rotunda towers stood proudly at the front gate, their slim structure reminding Amber of the story of *Rapunzel* from her childhood. Her dad had read it to her as a small child. She would curl up in his lap and listen as he told how Rapunzel unwound her long hair and lowered it to her prince.

She wondered briefly if her dad was safe, or if he even suspected that she had been missing for two weeks. They hadn't been getting along for a while, and it upset Amber to think about the fights. They had been spending less and less time together. Of course, the discovery that he had been dating an evil necromancer hadn't helped Amber's anxiety. When her curse had lifted, the missing pieces of her life had rushed forward like a tsunami. She had always disliked her *step-mother*, but when she found out that Patricia was the one who had placed a curse on her family, it had strengthened her hatred for the woman who had replaced her mother for ten years.

CONNOR SECURED his pack on his shoulder and swung in the direction of the woodland village that they were temporarily calling home. She grabbed her bag and readied herself to follow, when movement outside the castle brought her to a sudden stop.

'Connor!' she hissed, 'the gates are opening.'

They quickly sank to the ground and lay flat on the moss-covered floor. When they were sure that they hadn't been spotted, they crawled through the undergrowth until they were on the edge of the wooded area. The thick forest rose above the dirt road on a slight embankment. Twisted ferns clung to the sloping sides, trailing onto the dusty track. The thick vegetation kept the pair hidden from view as they watched the golden gates creak open. A battered carriage approached from the west heading for the open gates. Two jet black horses guided it down the track, their hooves leaving a cloud of dust in the air.

'They're in a hurry,' Connor nodded towards the castle, 'and they've got a welcoming party.'

Amber's eyes were hard as she watched Queen Alia's sister emerge from the cover of the towers. Nikita was nowhere near as beautiful as Alia. They shared the same creamy skin tone and sharp bone structure, but Nikita's face held no warmth, and the set of her mouth reflected her cruel nature. Her long white hair hung down her back, illuminated against the dark clothing she wore. Her midnight blue dress clung to her slim figure and brushed along the floor as she walked. The high collar made her neck look exceptionally long. She wore a crown of black obsidian and diamonds. Her wings were silver, with sharp angles and jagged edges, in contrast to Alia's delicate wings.

THE PRINCESS was flanked by two minotaurs as she approached the carriage, their spears pointing at the occupants of the wagon.

Connor inched forward, but Amber held him back as a second Hackney approached. There were six horses pulling the load, their legs buckling under the weight as their coats shone with sweat. A faerie warrior ferociously whipped at the smallest of the horses as it stumbled. Amber could make out the bowed tendons on its legs as it struggled along. Her hands began to tingle, and she could feel the heat rising up inside her as she regarded the white-haired fae who beat the animal.

Connor, as if sensing her rising power, laid his hand on her arm to calm her emotions.

'We have to pick our fights, Amber; this isn't one we can win.'

She nodded curtly, but she continued to watch the warrior. His white hair was scraped back from his face that was all square angles and angry expressions. The faintest hint of a scar caressed his forehead. Amber imprinted the horse-whipping faerie's image on her mind should they ever meet again.

The larger wagon was wooden and bound in thick iron strips. It had a canvas taupe stretched across the roof, but the back was open. Because it was dark inside the cart, she couldn't see what cargo the horses were struggling to pull.

The princess left the smaller coach and made her way to the faerie warrior. He fell to one knee and bowed his head in greeting. Nikita smiled and stroked his hair as she spoke quietly to him. When he eventually stood up, he was also smiling. The princess pulled him close and kissed him passionately.

'Now *that's* interesting,' Connor said softly. 'Our evil princess has a boyfriend.'

'I want to see what's on the wagon.' Ignoring the scene before her, Amber crawled a little farther through the ferns until she could get a better angle. She stopped, parallel to the back of the cart and gasped.

'What do you think it is?' Connor asked as he settled low in the ferns beside her.

She pointed at the opening and noticed that her hand shook. 'It's big, whatever it is.'

IN THE inky blackness of the wagon's interior, they could see two bright-red eyes. The silhouette of a huge beast filled the space. Nikita approached the back of the cart and laughed as she peered inside. She clapped her hands together and congratulated the warrior with another embrace. The carriage shook as its occupant tried to free itself. Bound by chains, it only managed to startle the horses with its stifled movements.

'To the castle!' Nikita exclaimed, instructing the minotaurs to move the heavy load forward. The horses panted hard and fast as they manoeuvred the cart between the towers.

Connor scrambled up the nearest tree. Like a well-trained monkey, he swung from branch to branch until he was high enough to see inside the castle courtyard. Amber tilted her head back to watch him as he rose higher. When he stopped, she saw the startled expression on his face.

'What is it?' she hissed up to him. 'Can you see it?'

He nodded and beckoned her to follow him up the tree. She reached for the first bough and swung herself up. She carefully moved from limb to limb until Connor extended a hand to help her up the last few branches. She nestled next to him and glanced over the outer wall of the castle.

From this height, they could see into the inner bailey. Fruit trees ran around the edge of a grassed courtyard, with a row of windows from the keep looking out over the centre. A fountain had once dominated the middle of the courtyard, but it now stood in ruins. The ornate mosaics that had decorated the stones were scattered across the grass. Amber's eyes travelled over the cluster of minotaurs brandishing their spears and rested on the creature that lay bound and muzzled. The canvas taupe had been pulled back to reveal the prisoner.

'A dragon!' Her heart hammered inside her chest as she watched Nikita's soldiers goad and taunt the beast. It strained against the chains that held its mighty wings bound, but they just cut deeper into its tough, chalky hide, drawing blood. 'Connor, we have to help it.'

'I know, but we can't do it on our own. We need Redka's and Alia's warriors.'

'Maybe I could use my powers?' She glanced down at her hands that were now tingling so violently that they vibrated. 'I could try and break its chains.'

Connor looked at her hands and shook his head, 'I'm sorry, Amber, but your powers are too unstable. What if you killed the dragon by accident? You'd never forgive yourself. I promise you, we *will* come back and free it.'

Frustration bubbled through her. Her seven powers had unlocked, but all she had been told by her mother, by Alia and even the ancient oracle Lavanya, was that she must not use them until she could control them. How was she supposed to control them if she couldn't practise using them?

Crossing her arms across her chest, she sat back on the tree branch and studied the castle. Why had Nikita caught a dragon? What use was such a huge creature to the princess if she couldn't tame it?

SHE REMEMBERED a brief conversation with Redka when he had tried to explain to her about the different realms. The dragon realm lay far to the north of Avaveil, and the Lost Lands of the necromancers were located in the south. Each realm was a separate entity and could only be accessed using the gateways. They had travelled through the fiery gateway to Phelan when they rescued Tom from the Guardians, and then escaped to Avaveil via a make-shift portal Redka had created. If Nikita had taken this dragon from its realm, then her soldiers would have had to come through a gateway. Not an easy task with such a cumbersome prisoner.

'Why do you suppose Nikita kidnapped a dragon?'

'I can't imagine,' Connor said. 'She could just be collecting a trophy for her wall like a hunter or she has plans to ransom it for something she needs.'

Of course. Nikita had stripped all the natural resources from Avaveil to pay for her minotaur army, burning woodland villages, and driving the fae deeper into the woods. Her jealousy for Queen Alia had manifested into a pure hatred of her people, and she spent years selling off the jewels, minerals, and even the children of the land to fund her materialistic lifestyle. Her parties at the castle were legendary, according to the lord of the village where they were living. She entertained necromancers and thieves and murderers from the human world. She surrounded herself with creatures from every realm but her own.

'The boyfriend!' Amber sat upright, nearly toppling from her perch. 'He's a faerie.'

'Yeah, I noticed that.' Connor studied her for a moment as he tried to understand the track of her thoughts.

'She *never* surrounds herself with the fae folk, ever!'

'So why is lover boy different?' Connor left his question hanging in the air as the smaller cart rocked into motion and entered the castle gates.

They could see Nikita and the white-haired warrior cuddled to-gether under the shade of an apple tree, surveying their prize with greedy anticipation. The minotaurs continued to harass the dragon, and the poor beast tried repeatedly to snap at its tormentors.

A HOODED figure descended from the small cart and wound its way through the throng of the hairy army until it reached Nikita's side. Lowering itself to the floor, it kissed the princess on the hand. The princess's smile was wicked as she raised her eyes to the wagon. Amber followed her gaze and saw a bundle of cloth on the floor of the cart. She was about to quiz Connor on what he thought it could be when the hooded figure spun around. The hood slipped back to reveal long blonde hair and a face Amber knew very well.

She clamped her hands over her mouth to stifle a scream as she watched Princess Nikita laugh and joke with the woman who had ruined her life. The woman who had cursed her family. The woman who had taken her father. Patricia.

CHAPTER 2

The branches scratched at her face as she ran through the woods. Her initial instinct had been to rush the castle gates and demand that the minotaurs hand over Patricia. It had taken Connor's very best half-fae magic to calm her rage, and yet she could feel her powers itching for release just below the surface of her skin.

Connor had wanted to stay and gather more information, but Amber couldn't stomach looking at that woman for a moment longer, not without driving the pointed end of a sword through her chest. For fear of her doing something stupid, Connor gave up and left his lookout point to accompany her to the woodland village.

'Slow down Amber.' He reached for her arm but she shrugged him off with a wave, in a flash he was launched skywards and crashed down amongst a patch of bracken ten feet away. A shocked gasp escaped his lips as he hit the floor.

'Connor!' She ran to his side and knelt next to him. He was bleeding from a gash on his forehead but appeared to have all his bones intact. 'I'm so sorry, I...I don't know how I did that.'

He lifted himself to a sitting position and looked directly into Amber's eyes.

'Lavanya told you that your powers were linked to your emotions. You have to control your feelings if you're going to have any luck with whatever it is you're capable of. We now know that throwing people through the air is a skill.'

Amber laughed with relief and slumped against a tree trunk. 'I've always kept my feelings in check, ask Tom. But here, here it's so different. It's like every fibre in my body is on fire, and if I don't expel it then it will burn me up from the inside.'

'Does Myanna have any information she can share? She's supposed to be descended from the oracles too?'

'I asked, she told me that her dominant oracle skill was her ability with spells and healing and my dad's inherited skill was his knowledge of witchcraft and the ancient ways. Not very helpful I'm afraid.'

They sat in silence for a while, listening to the sounds of the forest. Small unseen animals rustled through the undergrowth around them as the birds settled in their nests up high. As night crept by it coated the sky with stars.

'It's beautiful here isn't it?' Amber lay back watching the canopy of leaves wavering above them.

'I guess, I'm sure it was better when Alia ruled. The castle would have looked more homely then.'

Amber laughed, 'Redka told me that once Alia sits on her throne, the moat will fill with water and the wildflowers will grow along its banks again.'

'Sounds a bit too girly for my tastes,' Connor huffed.

'He also told me that the fae warriors would circle the castle and bind their magic to raise a wall of protection.'

'Now that sounds more like it. Warriors and magic are more fitting for a half-fae shop assistant.' His voice trailed off to a whisper.

Amber rolled over onto her side to look up at him. 'I'm sure India is fine Connor. She understood that we had to travel to Avaveil. It was her coven who couldn't re-open the gateway from Phelan, remember.'

'I know, I just miss her I guess. You've got your mum here, and Tom and I feel…I feel lonely.' He picked aimlessly at the bracken on the floor as his head hung low.

Amber wanted to offer him some comfort, but as she leaned forward to stroke his hair a crippling pain shot through her stomach. She fell backwards, curling herself into a tight ball.

'Amber! What's wrong?'

She clenched her teeth and folded her arms tightly across herself. The pain rocked through her in waves and then, just as swiftly as it had arrived, it was gone. She collapsed to the floor panting. Beads of sweat shone on her skin as she pressed her head to the forest floor. The leaves were cooling, and it didn't take her long to recover. Connor rubbed his hand along her spine in a comforting gesture.

'I'm okay,' she managed to say. 'Whatever it was, it's gone now.'

'Have you had these pains before?' His voice filled with concern; he had never seen Amber in such a state before.

'A couple of times,' she said sheepishly. 'They started when we arrived in Avaveil.'

'Does your mum know?'

'No, and Connor, I don't want her to know. You can't tell anyone.'

'Why not?'

'They'll tell me it's because of Redka.' She stood up and dusted her trousers before retrieving her bag. 'Ever since Myanna and Alia healed him I've been told to give him space, and that he can't see me yet as it will weaken his powers. But, the more I stay away from him, the worse it gets for me.'

Connor eyed her incredulously, 'Are you telling me that the two of you are connected *physically* as in, if he hurts, you hurt and all that mojo?'

'I don't know for certain. I'm not sure if we experience each other's pain, but I have a terrible feeling of dread when I'm away from him. I think this has manifested as a physical pain.'

'Does Redka feel it?'

'I don't know, they won't let me near him. They tell me it's too dangerous.' She paused for a long moment before speaking again. 'You could speak to him, find out if he's suffering too. It may help Alia and my mother to see reason and let us be together. Please Connor, I beg you.'

Connor flung his pack over his shoulder and started walking, his heavy boots crushing the ferns underfoot as he worked his way through the trees to the woodland village. His silence hung in the air as they travelled until eventually, on the outskirts of the village, he turned to face her.

'I'll ask him, but if I find out that the two of you need to stay apart for your safety, then Amber, I will do everything in my power to make that happen.' Then he walked away.

THE CIRCULAR room in the woodland lord's treehouse was warm and comfortable. Amber watched the village come to life from the open window as the sun crept above the treeline. Fae warriors set out in scouting packs, vanishing into the undergrowth of the surrounding forest. Children bustled back and forth between the tiny bakery and the lord's house with bread and cakes for the assembled group.

She sensed his presence even before the door opened. A tingle of energy vibrated up from her feet and settled in the pit of her stomach. She held her hands out in front of her convinced they would be glowing bright red.

When Redka opened the door, his eyes locked on hers, and his handsome face lit up in a wide smile. The sun reflected off his long white hair which hung loose over his shoulder. One warning look from Myanna kept her rooted to the spot, but she ached to run at him and feel his warm embrace. He moved quickly to the seat next to Amber and before Myanna could disapprove, he planted a lingering kiss on Amber's forehead.

'How are you feeling?' she asked, with the knowing look of someone who had shared the wrath of General Loso's fury when they escaped from Phelan. He had nearly died. She came close to death herself but managed to vanquish the Guardian General, with a little help from the realm demons. She still hadn't shared the experience with Connor, Tom or even her mother. She had frightened herself with the ferocity of her power.

'I am fine and back to full strength. How are you coping in my realm?' His eyes twinkled when he spoke.

Amber smiled, 'I feel like I'm going slightly mad, but I'm happy about it as the location is so beautiful.'

Redka laced his fingers with hers and squeezed her hand. Myanna cleared her throat as she looked on.

'What?' Amber hissed at her mother, 'What exactly are you afraid of? We're holding hands not blowing up the forest.'

'It's for your own safety Amber. We understand that you both suffered a terrible fright back in Phelan but it's important that we work with your powers without any distractions.' Myanna patted her daughter's hand as she spoke.

Amber felt the anger rise in her chest as Redka tugged at her hand, but before she could comprehend her actions she was standing over her mother.

'A terrible fright!' She shouted it loud enough to silence the small room and draw everyone's attention. 'A terrible fright is finding a spider in your shoe or realising you've lost your house key. What happened to me and Redka in Phelan was *not* a fright; it was beyond terrifying. I watched Loso run a sword through his chest before turning on me. I had to pull powers from the bowels of that hell dimension to survive. I didn't ask for any of this.' She waved her arms in a wide arc before noticing that all eyes were on her.

Redka rose from his chair and wrapped his arm around her shoulder. Her resolve faltered as she laid her forehead against his arm and breathed in his woodland scent.

'Everything is going to be fine Amber; I am here to help you.'

She looked up into the purple hue of his eyes and marvelled at how bold and powerful he was again. He had fully healed, with no signs of any lasting damage. So why wasn't she feeling better? Why did she have a deep foreboding about her future here in Avaveil?

'I know Redka, and I wish it were that easy, but my mother and Alia have other plans. I believe they think I'm a danger to you.' She stepped away from him still looking into his calming eyes. 'Until I can prove them wrong then we need to stay away from each other.'

She kissed the ends of her fingertips and pressed them against his lips before hurrying from the room.

Tom was working with a small group of fae children on how to hold a sword when she reached the ground. Their faces shone with excitement as they parried and thrust their make-shift willow branch weapons at each other.

'Good, that's good,' Tom encouraged them as he straightened their shoulders and adjusted their stance. He slapped a young fae girl on the shoulder as he walked past, 'Star student Dawni.' She beamed up at him before attacking her partner once more.

Tom nodded at Amber as she approached, 'Hey cutie, has the big meeting finished already?'

She shook her head, 'No, I walked out, but not before I totally embarrassed myself and shouted at my mother.'

Tom laughed loudly, 'That's my Amber.'

'It's not funny Tom. I'm losing my mind in this place. When have I ever lost my temper before?'

Tom roared with laughter at this and clutched his sides as if his innards were in danger of falling out. 'Oh, I don't know, maybe every time Patricia opened her mouth, or all the times your Dad grounded you, or when…'

'Okay, okay I get your point.' She held up her hand to stop him from talking but couldn't help grinning as Tom wiped the tears from his eyes.

'In all seriousness Amber, you haven't lost your mind. You've just found out you're supernatural with all sorts of funky powers to contend with. I, for one, think you're doing a great job.'

She nodded and kicked absentmindedly at a stone on the floor. She was unsure if she had the same amount of faith in her abilities as her best friend did, but she was grateful for the support. If only her mother could be as supportive.

'Is there any news of Nikita?' Tom dragged her from her thoughts.

All they had heard since their arrival in Avaveil were stories of the horror and destruction that Alia's sister had rained down on the faerie realm in her absence.

Queen Alia's sudden disappearance at the hands of General Loso had been the perfect stage for Princess Nikita to dig her claws into Avaveil and bleed it dry. She had mourned for her sister, but gave up her pretence swiftly to take her place on the throne.

'The scouts can only confirm that she is still in the castle with her faerie boyfriend and that Patricia hasn't left her side.'

'You see that's the bit I don't understand.' Tom rested his back against the bark of a huge sweet chestnut tree as he spoke, 'What the hell is Patsy doing here in Avaveil?'

'I wish I knew. She was very friendly with Nikita, so I assume this isn't her first visit. I want to know that my dad's safe. That bitch could have him locked in another dimension of hell, or worse.' Her voice trailed off to a whisper, 'She might have killed him when we disappeared to Phelan. I just wish I could have got my hands on her.' Amber bunched her hands into fists as she spoke, and the floor trembled beneath them.

Tom jumped away from the tree with a startled cry, 'Earthquake!'

'It's not an earthquake Tom; it's me.' She held her palms out for him to look.

He grasped her hands in his and pulled her into a tight hug.

'It's going to be okay. We'll work this out together, I promise you.' He kissed the top of her head, and they stayed wrapped in each other's arms for a long while.

A commotion close to the village centre pulled them from their companionable silence. The scouting group had returned, and from the ruckus it was causing, Amber knew the information had to be important.

The meeting in the lord's house had disbanded and as they approached Amber could see Alia and Connor in deep conversation with Mags, the leader of the group. His cropped white hair shone in the dappled sunlight as he gestured wildly with his arms.

'Looks serious,' Tom murmured as they reached the outskirts of the group. His attention was deflected momentarily by an attractive fae warrior called Cass, who gave him a wink as she passed by them. Amber smiled to herself as she watched Tom turn a deep shade of crimson.

'I don't understand what she could be doing.' Alia was saying, 'It doesn't make any sense, the realm leaders are our allies, not our enemies.'

Amber nudged Connor's elbow as she came to a stop beside him. 'What's going on?'

'Mags and Cass have just returned from their last scout, and it appears our princess has acquired a few more trophies.' Connor raised his eyebrows as he looked down at Amber.

'You mean trophies like the dragon?'

'Yes, except this time she's added the leader of the water sprites and the head of the orc realm.'

'That's a high profile collection. Do we know if the dragon we saw is important?'

Connor nodded sharply, 'Turns out that the white dragon is called Roth, and just so happens to be the king of the dragon realm.'

Queen Alia began pacing on the spot as she spoke with Mags and the village lord. Her worries were clearly etched across her beautiful face.

'What's she going to do?' Amber nodded in Alia's direction.

'There was talk of a raiding party. Taking a small group and breaking into the castle for information. Purely reconnaissance.'

'Which fool agreed to do that?'

Connor smiled and shrugged his muscular shoulders.

'Connor you didn't?'

'It's important that we find out what Nikita's doing if we have any chance of helping Alia reclaim the castle. It was the right thing to do.'

Amber mulled this over for a while as she watched Mags giving orders to the fae warriors. She could see Tom through the crowds with his head bent in private conversation with Cass. Myanna was attending to a child with an insect bite; her healing balms cluttered around her feet as she worked.

Everyone had a role within the village. Everyone except her. She was the loose cannon that was one bad mood away from exploding and levelling the village.

'I'm coming.' She folded her arms across her chest and looked at Connor pointedly.

If she was expecting an argument she was mistaken, Connor let out a short snort of laughter. 'I thought you might.'

AMBER LEFT the warriors to go over the plans for their little mission. She hadn't quite got over the effects of the last expedition she'd jumped at, but this time she had the opportunity to find answers about her father.

As she wandered through the forest, she allowed the peace and quiet of the woods to soak into her bones. The sunlight flickered through the leaves leaving wavering patterns on the ground beneath her. She ran her hands over the tall ferns trying to concentrate her energies on feeling the plants essence. Myanna had told her that all living things were made up of energy and she needed to learn to tune into this to calm her emotions.

Closing her eyes, she stopped walking and practised her grounding meditation. It had taken time to master the feeling of being rooted to the earth, but now that she could feel it, the sensation gave her a deep sense of calm.

As she allowed her body to relax, she could feel her skin begin to heat up. Not in a fiery brimstone kind of way, but as a warm sensation that flooded through her muscles and limbs. It was the closest she had felt to bliss since landing in Avaveil. After the magical faerie circle had spat her and Redka out in a bloody heap, she had thought that any form of happiness had been removed from her life entirely.

Tilting her face to the sky she let the warmth of the sun caress her skin. Her mind was cleared of all thoughts, and she concentrated on the sound of the leaves rustling in the breeze. She could hear the birds chirping high in the over locking branches of the trees. She could smell the sweet scent of jasmine.

Her heart hammered in her chest as she took a deep breath. Jasmine didn't grow in this part of the forest. Slowly she opened her eyes.

'Redka.' She softly whispered his name, afraid that if she spoke too loudly he would be taken away again.

He held a finger up to his lips to silence her, and then jerked his head to the side, gesturing her to follow him. They wound their way through the forest in silence until eventually coming to a large overhanging willow tree.

Redka scooped the long branches to the side to reveal a make-shift room. Long willow sticks had been interwoven to form the walls that were hidden from view by the curtain of leaves that stretched out far and wide to touch the ground.

Moving through the small opening Amber took in her surroundings. The thick trunk of the tree dominated the centre, and a low bench ran around its circumference. Bright cushions covered the seat, making it an inviting place to rest. To the right was a blanket spread across the forest floor where a picnic of fruits and bread had been laid out.

On the left, running around the edge of the willow wall was a row of wooden chests. The nearest one was open, and Amber could see clothes spilling over the rim.

'What is this place?' She slowly spun full circle taking in every tiny detail. 'It's beautiful.'

Redka smiled and motioned for her to join him on the blanket. He picked up a red apple and polished it on his tunic.

'This is our special place,' he said. 'Ever since I recovered, I've felt like a piece of me was missing. When I asked my mother if I could see you, she told me you were unwell, and I had to leave you to rest. So I filled my time building this for when you got better.'

Amber's eyes filled with tears. 'It's the most beautiful place I've ever seen.'

'I'm glad you like it and I hope it makes you feel better.'

'Redka, I wasn't ill. Alia and Myanna told me the same about you. I wasn't allowed to see you because they thought I'd be a danger to you. I missed you so much.'

Redka pulled her onto his lap, and she wrapped her arms tightly around his neck. He smoothed her hair and kissed her neck.

'It appears our mothers have been meddling in our affairs.'

Amber laughed and reached for an apple. 'I'm sure they think they're doing the right thing, but I don't understand why they get so nervous when we're together. I haven't hurt you.'

'Of course you haven't hurt me. You saved my life.'

'Myanna said my powers are linked to my emotions and that you distract me.'

Redka kissed her jaw line, 'I don't know how they could think I would distract you.'

'Hmm…no, not a clue.' She giggled and lowered her lips to meet his.

Redka cupped her face in his warm hands and kissed her deeply. Her head swam as his fae magic seeped into her. She pressed her body close to his and lost herself in their embrace. For the first time in what seemed like forever, she felt like a normal girl again.

Reluctantly, they broke apart but Amber stayed nestled in the safety of his arms.

'Will you help me to control my powers?' She moved her head so she could look up at him, and felt an enormous relief when she saw the pride in his face.

'I would be honoured.' He bowed his head slightly. 'I think it may be wise if we keep it a secret from our family though. Judging by their efforts to keep us apart I guess they would not approve of our arrangement.'

'Agreed,' Amber said. 'Can we meet here every day? This place seems to bring out the best in me.'

Redka chuckled and hugged her tightly. 'I think that is a wise move.'

CHAPTER 3

The swirling white cloud cleared and Lavanya stood in her shimmering white gown in front of Amber. The oracle eye pendant glistened on her chest as she beckoned for Amber to approach.

'Welcome little eye, it has been some time since we talked.'

'Arriving in Avaveil was a bit of a shock to the system, and getting my head around the oracle stuff has taken time,' she confessed.

'You have no need to explain yourself to me, little eye. From what I see, you are doing well with your lessons. Myanna is teaching you well.'

'Yes, I guess.' Amber wondered briefly if the all-seeing oracle knew about her extracurricular lessons with Redka. As if sensing her trepidation, Lavanya reached over to pat Amber's hand.

'I understand your apprehension, but you have nothing to fear from me. You and Redka are bound together for a greater good. You were destined to meet and to free Queen Alia so she could be returned to her rightful realm, just as you were to be reunited with your mother. Neither I nor my fellow oracles foresaw your bond with the faerie prince lasting beyond Phelan.'

'What does that mean? Everyone is trying to keep us apart, but it hurts...literally.' Amber pressed her hands against her stomach at the faint memory of the agony that plagued her.

Lavanya watched her with interest. 'You feel his pain?'

'I don't know what I feel, but when I don't see him I get horrific stomach cramps like I've been stabbed with a sharp sword.'

'Does he experience this discomfort?'

'I haven't asked him.'

Lavanya closed her eyes and raised her hands to the sky. She began to chant under her breath, quietly at first, but growing louder and louder until she was almost shouting.

Amber pressed her palms to her ears as she watched the white clouds oscillate.

As Lavanya reached her crescendo, three figures appeared from the clouds, two men and a woman. They were dressed in long robes: the woman wore silver, one man wore pale blue, and the third, a tall man with jet black hair, wore a golden robe edged in blood red rubies.

Lavanya embraced each of the oracles in turn before approaching Amber.

'Little eye, the time has come for you to understand your heritage and the destiny that has been bestowed upon you. May I introduce Kavi, my brother and the oracle of stealth.'

A thin man advanced and thrust his hand forward to lay his palm on Amber's head.

He moved with a speed and grace that startled Amber, but before she could react he had moved beyond her and was now bowing deeply in greeting.

'An honour to meet you, little eye.'

Amber's head thumped, and her eyes took time to focus. 'What have you done to me?'

'I have gifted you with stealth my child. I have activated all of your senses for you to navigate your world. It still shocks me how the humans rely so much on belief, rather than instinct.' He chuckled to himself as if lost in a private joke that was centuries old.

'Err, thank you.' Amber wasn't sure if a simple thank you was sufficient when receiving a gift from an ancient oracle, but it was all she had.

Lavanya ushered a petite woman with curly silver hair forward. She curtseyed to Amber. 'My name is Devi,' she said softly, 'If I may, I would like to gift you with glamour.'

Amber looked to Lavanya for guidance and was happy to see her oracle guide was smiling.

'Thank you, I accept.' Amber bowed her head waiting for Devi to lay her hand on the top of her head. Instead, the tiny oracle shifted and changed right before her eyes; her body evaporating into a silver fog that descended to coat Amber's skin. She could feel a weightless sensation overtake her and then as abruptly as it began, it faded away, and Devi was standing before her once more.

Before she could recover herself fully from her encounter with Devi, she found herself face to face with the tall man in the golden robe.

His hair was as black as obsidian and was a harsh contrast to the serene surroundings of Lavanya's cloud. He stared at Amber with hard eyes and made no move to introduce himself. Amber stood her ground and squared her shoulders, standing up to her full five feet and seven inches. She nodded her head at the imposing oracle and offered her hand to him. 'My name is Amber Noble,' she said. 'I am your descendant. Your great-great-great-one-thousand-times-removed-granddaughter.'

The giant man's face broke into a wide grin, and he began to laugh. He laughed until his shoulders shook and tears streamed down his face. Eventually he accepted Amber's hand and shook it vigorously.

'I like her!' he said, talking to Lavanya.

'I like you!' he turned to Amber still shaking her hand, 'You have a fire in your belly and a warrior's heart. I am Isha. I'm your great-great-great-whatever.' He laughed again as he finally released Amber's hand. She rubbed her fingers to get the circulation flowing again.

Lavanya shook her head as she took Isha's arm. 'Always the joker my brother.'

'Ah yes, but as the oracle of strength and war I need a good chuckle every millennia or so.'

'War!' Amber was stunned. 'Why would you need an oracle of war? Surely the ancient oracles are against fighting and want peace. Isn't that

why you scattered to the four corners, because us humans wanted war and greed?'

'You know your history, little eye,' Isha said, his voice booming across the silvery clouds. 'I don't campaign for war; I simply use my skills to aid the generals and warriors to a peaceful finale. My gift of strength helps keep order in many of the realms.'

'It hasn't kept the peace in Avaveil,' she said curtly.

Isha levelled a stern gaze on Amber as he spoke. 'Princess Nikita is a law unto herself. My powers are beyond the reach of a necromancer's magic.'

'Are you talking about Patricia? Is she doing magic for Nikita?' Amber longed for answers and could almost taste the victory of ending Patricia's evil reign against her family.

'You have a strong amount of rage for such a tiny person, little eye. Maybe having my gift of strength and fighting isn't wise.'

Amber crossed her arms over her chest and looked up at Isha. 'The necromancer you talk about has done plenty of harm to my family, and if I want to stop her then that's my business. I don't need extra strength to do it.'

'I think you will need all the strength you can get for what is coming.'

'What do you mean? Do you know something?' Amber suddenly felt very small and insignificant. This huge oracle of a man who towered over her stepped back and moved to engage his brother and sisters, leaving Amber feeling deflated.

She was about to ask Isha to explain himself, when suddenly a crippling pain shot through her body sending her sprawling to the ground. She screamed out as the intensity increased and took her breath away.

The oracles rushed to her side. Luvanya scooped her head off the floor and rested it in her lap, smoothing her hand across Amber's forehead. She cried out again; the pain was too much to handle. It had never been this bad before.

'When I'm away from Redka, I feel this pain.' She spat the words out through gritted teeth, willing them to understand. But as she watched the shifting expressions on their faces, she began to think that maybe she was wrong.

Isha knelt beside her. 'This pain is not linked to your prince, little eye. It is much closer to home.' He unbuttoned his golden robe to reveal his chest and abdomen. There were deep scars running across his skin; some were old, but a couple looked fresh and raw.

'I experience every injury and pain that my descendants go through. My strength and immortality give me the power to survive these ordeals. Unfortunately, my family is not always as fortunate.' He pointed to the deepest of the old scars. 'This was my son's punishment for not joining with the warlords of the East. They gutted him and left him to die in the desert.' He pointed to a fresh scar that still bled. It ran from just below his left collarbone down to his belly button. 'This just happened, to another descendant of mine; a strong leader who until recently was kept out of my reach by dark magic.'

'What do you mean, it just happened?' Amber asked, gradually recovering her strength as her pain lessened.

Isha placed his big hand on her shoulder and leaned in closer. 'At the same time you cried out in pain, I felt the cut of the knife blade on my skin. We are linked to the same person in our blood line. We both feel their pain.'

He waited for Amber to understand, watching her face with a quiet patience as she put the pieces together.

Her eyes flew wide as the realisation hit her. Isha nodded and gave her a sad smile.

'I give you my gift of strength and fighting, little eye. You are going to need it.'

AMBER RAN through the forest blindly as the branches ripped at her face. She ploughed through the trees without a care for the lacerations on her cheeks and arms. Redka had left her to sleep in the willow tree when he returned to check in with Alia and the warriors. It had been hard to break free from her encounter with Lavanya and the ancient oracles. Normally, when she visited the oracle realm, there was a friendly face to greet her when she awoke, but today she was unprepared and alone.

She spotted Myanna first when she broke through the treeline and hurried to her side before collapsing on her knees.

'Goodness Amber, what is it?' Myanna grabbed her healer's bag and began rooting through the potions as she looked at the cuts on her daughter's face.

'We have to get to the castle,' she panted, 'I need to find Patricia.'

'Yes, yes Connor told me about the mission. I'm not sure it's such a good idea that you go with them though.' She dabbed a sticky green substance to the cut under Amber's left eye. 'The fae are better equipped to cope.'

Amber slapped her mother's hand away and grabbed her by the shoulders. 'I'm going to the castle, mum, because I'm the *only* person equipped to cope with what we will find there.'

'What do you mean? Amber, what's going on?' Her brow creased as she watched her daughter struggle to find the right words.

'I've spoken to the oracles. Spoken to all of them. They've given me their gifts of stealth, glamour and strength, so I'll be fine. But mum, I need Redka's help.'

'No!' Myanna jumped to her feet and began packing her potions away. 'It's not safe for the two of you to be together, Amber. The oracles were wrong to give you these gifts when you can't even manage the powers you have. You are ruled by your emotions and Alia has seen...' She trailed off as if realising she had said too much.

'Alia has seen what exactly?' Amber stood up slowly and eyeballed her mother.

'Since we returned to Avaveil, Alia's visions have been returning stronger and clearer. She could foresee certain outcomes when we were in Phelan, but her power was greatly reduced. She saw that a warrior would rescue us from Phelan, but she couldn't have known it would be you. Now that we are home, and her visions are back to full strength, she believes it is imperative that you and Redka are kept apart.'

'Why? What happens if we don't stay away from each other?'

'She has sensed it, Amber. She said that the warrior will harm the prince. What am I supposed to do? She is my queen, and I trust her.'

Amber was quiet for a long moment before she answered. 'Alia is not *my* queen and Avaveil is not *my* home. She says that a warrior will harm Redka, and yet I don't call myself one, and have *never* considered myself to be a warrior. She has no proof that I will harm her son, but she insists on keeping us apart when we are stronger together. I'm going to find out what happened to my dad, and then I'm going to find a way to get me, Tom, and Connor to our real home in the human world.' She walked away without a second glance.

CONNOR FOUND her brooding in the apple orchard twenty minutes later, and flopped down on the ground beside her.

'Your mum sent me to check on you,' he said.

'You can tell Myanna to leave me the hell alone.'

'I don't think I want to tell an all-powerful witch to leave anything the hell alone, especially her daughter. What's going on?'

Amber sighed and recounted the spat with her mother, filling in the gaps with her thoughts and interpretations on the matter.

'For the record, I spoke to Redka and he hasn't suffered from any separation pains.'

Amber nodded as she picked at a blade of grass, 'He wouldn't. It isn't Redka's pain I'm feeling.'

'If it isn't linked to Redka, then who?'

Amber lifted her face to look at Connor, her eyes shining with unshed tears, 'It's my dad.'

Connor rested his arms on his knees and lowered his voice, 'Are you sure?'

'Yes, I've met the oracles and Isha confirmed it. He's linked to my dad too, because we all share a bloodline.'

'Isha? Who the hell is Isha?'

Amber rested her head back against the apple tree and smiled, 'Remember when you showed me that picture of the ancient oracles back in India's shop?'

He nodded, 'The guys sitting on the cloud with all the scrolls?'

'Yes, well I got to meet them, all of them. My mum is a descendant of Lavanya, which is why she's my guide. Dad is the descendant of Isha, who just happens to be the oracle of strength and war.'

'Well, that's handy under the circumstances. Does he plan on giving us a helping hand?'

'They don't leave the oracle realm, but they did pass on their gifts to me. I guess I just have to work out how to use them.'

'Gifts! As in more oracle powers?'

'Don't panic Connor, I'm not going to blow anything else up. Lavanya is helping me to work with the powers I have and Red...' she stopped herself before revealing too much about her recent meetings with Redka, 'Let's just say I've got all the help I need.'

She stood up and extended a hand to Connor, 'Come on, let's go find out when we leave for the castle. Mags should have the plans finalised by now.'

Connor watched her for a moment, before finally accepting her hand and jumping up from the ground. Before she could let go, he pulled her close, 'Be careful Amber,' he said.

CHAPTER 4

The small group nestled low in the undergrowth. Mags had hand-picked his best fae warriors for the mission and wordlessly instructed them to move left and right.

Cass headed up the left flank, taking her team swiftly through the forest and along the outskirts of the dirt track leading to the castle gates. The two minotaur guards remained oblivious to what was happening around them.

Mags waved his slender hand and gestured for Amber and Connor to follow his team to the right.

With the castle wall on her left side, Amber kept her head low and followed Connor as they weaved in and out of the forest towards the dried up moat. Alia had told them about a small trap door in the lower wall. Her father had added the door as a means of escape should the castle ever come under attack. It had never been used during his reign nor Alia's. She didn't know if it was still accessible, but it was their best tactic.

In the darkness of the night, the rich, buttery colour of the castle walls looked cold and grey. It was certainly not as inviting as the first time Amber had laid eyes on it. Her heart threatened to break free from her chest as she crawled on her belly through the tall grasses surrounding the base of the walls. Mags punched his fist into the air to stop the group. Amber clung to the earth and held her breath. A deep growl filled the air, followed by the sound of laughter.

Connor had crawled parallel to Amber and leaned in close to whisper in her ear, 'It's Roth. The guards are taunting him.'

Amber nodded, 'We have to help him.'

'Not tonight, this is purely reconnaissance, not a rescue mission. Stay close to me Amber.'

With that, Connor crawled forward. He pushed towards Mags, who was jerking his arms in all directions and sending the fae scattering along the perimeter. The female warriors spread their wings and shot up into the sky, like obsidian bullets. Amber strained to see them in the night sky, but with their black clothing and transparent wings, they blended with the stars.

Mags was ushering Amber forward. Using her elbows and knees, she shuffled towards him.

'The trap door is just ahead. When I open it, you and Connor will have just seconds to slip inside before I have to seal it again. We can't afford for the guards to notice anything amiss.'

Connor winked at Amber, 'Just like old times eh!'

She rolled her eyes.

THE TRAP door was hidden beneath the dried grass and bracken. Mags cleared the edges and found the latch. It opened with ease and Connor slipped through first, swiftly followed by Amber. The door closed behind them, and they were plunged into darkness.

'Now this is just like old times,' Amber hissed into the black void. She could hear Connor chuckle. Then, as he activated his crystal torch, a ghostly light appeared, hovering in mid-air.

'You could always activate your glow worm magic and guide the way.'

'Very funny. Knowing my luck I'll start a fire.'

Amber looked around the cramped space. There were stone steps in front of them that went higher than their witch light could illuminate.

'Shall we?' Connor swept a hand towards the stairs.

Amber took a deep breath and followed Connor, as he made his way up the stairwell.

She steadied herself on the stone walls, which were damp and smelt of dirty dishwater.

It didn't take them long to reach the top, where they entered a circular stone room. Stacked along the walls and in every available space were wooden crates filled with large glass jars. Connor lifted one of the containers out and held it up to the light.

'This is mugwort.' Connor extended the jar for Amber to see.

'So?'

'So, this is what the fae use for medicinal purposes. It's fresh so somebody must be using it. Someone of fae origin.'

'Nikita's fae boyfriend didn't look like a healer when we saw him on the road.' Amber remembered the white-haired warrior who had whipped the horses.

'No he didn't, unless...'

'Unless what?'

'It can also be used to bring about vivid dreams or intense hallucinations if it's burnt. It's possible they aren't using it for its healing properties.'

'If they kept this stuff burning would it keep someone in a constant dream state?'

'It's possible. There are enough jars here to put the entire realm into a dream state.'

'I guess we know how Nikita's managing to subdue a dragon then!'

THEY WORKED their way through the crates until they reached the door to the main part of the castle. With as much care as he could muster, Connor turned the handle and opened the door just enough so he could peep through.

'What do you see?' Amber asked, straining to look over his shoulder.

He opened the door a little wider, and stepped through into the space beyond. The flaming torches attached to golden sconces on the walls gave off a pale light that washed the area with a welcoming glow. The interior of the castle was not as scary as she had envisioned. They were at the end of a curved corridor which bent away to the left. They couldn't see beyond the end, but they could hear murmurs in the distance.

Connor inched forward, hugging his back to the wall as he moved quickly and quietly along the length of the corridor. Amber followed his every move, keeping as close to him as she could. As they reached the bend in the wall, Connor stopped and held out his arm to pin Amber back. The voices were louder here, a man and a woman.

'I've tried to extract the powers, but the subject is too strong. She is asking for the impossible,' said the female voice.

'Queen Nikita only asks for what she deserves. If you can't give her what she needs then she will have no further need for you.' The man's harsh voice echoed off the stone walls.

'She needs me Aaron, you and I both know that. I manipulated the greatest spell any necromancer has ever cast and brought her my prize. She will not turn on me.'

The man gave an empty, hollow laugh. 'If you don't get the dragon's powers soon, then trust me when I say that she *will* turn on you.'

'She has the essence of the water sprite and the orc. I've even drained the witch's power for her. Surely she can give me more time with the dragon?'

'I will speak with Nikita and see if she can give you the time you need, but Patricia, I must warn you. She will tire of your human toy soon enough, and you don't want to see her when she's bored.'

The man's footsteps reverberated off the stone walls as he walked away, ringing in Amber's ears as she processed the conversation they had overheard.

'They were talking about my dad,' she whispered in Connor's ear.

He nodded and pushed her backwards towards the round room.

'We have to get back to Mags and report in.' He pushed open the door to the store room and began to weave between the crates of mugwort. Once at the staircase he turned to usher Amber down in front of him. A blinding flash filled his vision, and something hit him hard in the centre of the chest. He lost his footing on the top step and fell, tumbling down the flight of stone stairs. As he thundered downwards, his head cracked against the rough walls and hot blood poured into his eyes. His ribs snapped as he landed with a crash at the bottom.

Looking up at the top of the steps he could make out Amber's silhouette against the backdrop of the candlelight. Someone was holding her by the hair as she struggled to free herself.

'Connor!' she shouted. It was the last thing he had heard before he blacked out.

AMBER'S ARMS ached where they had been suspended in chains attached to two stone pillars, and her head pounded where Patricia had hit her with the hilt of a sword. The guardhouse where she was being held smelt strong of wet dog, and it turned her stomach.

The hairy beasts who guarded her had taken turns to goad and harass her for the first hour, as she hung between the pillars. Her feet barely touched the floor, so she tried to balance on her tip toes to lessen the pain in her shoulder blades.

Fortunately, the guards soon tired of their new plaything and settled down to sleep on the flagstones. Dirty beds of straw littered the floor space, and each of the guards snored loudly as they slept around her.

Amber closed her eyes, but blinked them open quickly as the image of Connor's face resurfaced. She had heard the sickening crunch of his bones as he fell down the stairs into the inky blackness. She prayed that Mags had heard him fall and was able to get to him. If they rescued Connor, then it wouldn't be long before they came to rescue her.

The guardhouse door opened, and Amber flinched as Patricia walked in followed by the white-haired warrior from the road.

He approached Amber, kicking the minotaur guards out of his way as he walked. They grunted and shifted positions, cowering back from his path.

'I am Aaron of Avaveil, Queen Nikita's most loyal servant.'

Amber spat on the floor in front of him. 'Nikita is no queen. She sits on a stolen throne and surrounds herself with evil.' She looked pointedly at Patricia as she spoke.

Using the back of his hand, Aaron hit Amber hard across the face. Her head snapped back from the force. She recovered herself, licking the blood from her lip as she levelled her gaze on him. She could feel the energy flowing up through her limbs, building and building.

She channelled her thoughts until she could direct her power. It rushed down her arms and exploded from the palms of her hands. The chains on her arms shattered as if they were made of glass, and the minotaur guards jumped to their feet surrounding her with their spears at the ready.

Aaron stood his ground. 'Impressive. Patricia didn't tell me you were so powerful.'

'Patsy wouldn't know. She took my dad on a mini break, and we haven't had a chance to catch up yet.' Amber glared at Patricia, who hung back, using the hairy guards as protection.

Aaron smiled at her as he gestured towards Patricia. 'Please, be my guest. If you two need some girl time I can leave.'

'No! Aaron, for goodness sake shackle the girl.' Patricia paled visibly at Aaron's game.

Amber didn't waste any time, and centred her power to release a single fireball. She threw it at Patricia hitting her square in the face and setting her long blonde hair alight. Screaming as the flames engulfed her, she writhed around as the guards patted the fire out with heavy blankets.

Aaron clapped his hands slowly, and inclined his head in a sort of salute to Amber. He waved at the guards to remove the hysterical necromancer from the room, and they obeyed swiftly.

'Do I need to re-shackle you?' The fae warrior stood in front of Amber with his hand resting on the hilt of his sword.

'No, I just had an overwhelming urge to cause that woman pain. I feel much better now.'

Aaron chuckled, 'Patricia is a highly skilled necromancer who answers to the queen. I'm sure Nikita will be displeased with you.'

'I couldn't care less if *Princess* Nikita is displeased, I don't answer to anyone but myself.'

'Why are you so adamant that Nikita is not the queen of this realm?'

It was Amber's turn to smile, 'Because I arrived in Avaveil with the true queen, and with a little help from some friends, we plan on giving the throne back to Alia.'

From the look of shock on Aaron's face, he had no idea that Alia was alive, let alone here in Avaveil. While he was distracted, she acted quickly and snatched the sword from Aaron's scabbard. Holding it under his chin, she pressed hard enough to draw blood. She took a moment to enjoy seeing him flinch.

'Powerful *and* graceful. You impress me more and more.' He held his arms out in surrender.

'I'm not here to impress,' she snapped at him, 'I'm here to find out what Patricia has done with my father.'

'Maybe I can answer that question my dear.' Amber just had time to see Nikita enter the room before she was thrown into the air by magical energy and suspended from the ceiling.

Aaron bent down to retrieve his sword before bowing in front of Nikita. 'My queen, I apologise for my tardiness. I fear that I underestimated the girl.'

'Yes, yes, do not fear Aaron. Having seen the mess she made of my necromancer, I think you are not alone in underestimating her.'

'She has great power, my queen. She may be of use to you.'

'I will never work for you! I don't care what you do to me!' Amber shouted down from her position, struggling to break the magical bond that held her so tightly.

Nikita's cruel laugh sounded like nails being dragged down a chalkboard. 'My dear child, I don't want you to work for me. I merely want to take your power away and have it as my own.'

Amber's eyes widened.

'The water sprite and the orc. You've taken their power?'

Nikita clapped her hands together like a small excited child, 'Precisely my dear. They are powerful leaders with talents I can only dream of. With a little dark magic, my necromancer has found a way to extract this power and give it to me.'

'What about the dragon? What about Roth?'

Nikita's eyes hardened as she stared up at Amber, 'You seem to know an awful lot about my business. Why exactly are you here?'

Before she could answer, Aaron interrupted, 'She is here for her father. It appears this child is the offspring of the witch, Alan Noble.'

'Aaah then, we are practically family, my dear. Alan is enjoying the hospitality of my castle; I have invited him to stay here with me, but he does like to resist. It's a little game we play, but I'm sure he will come around to my way of thinking very soon.'

Nikita turned on her heel and made for the door. As she left, she flicked her hand to release the hold on Amber, and gave instructions to Aaron. 'Lock her up. I want Patricia to extract her powers at first light.'

Amber hit the floor hard and a sharp pain steamrolled through her brain. She tried to roll out of Aaron's grasp, but he was ready for her. He covered her nose and mouth with a rag laced with a pungent herb. She struggled briefly until the potion began to work, and the world spun away from her.

'HOW COULD you let this happen?' Redka paced the floor of the lodge while he tried to get a handle on the rage and fear that bubbled in the pit of his stomach.

'We were jumped from behind; neither of us saw it coming.' Connor nursed a cold compress to the side of his head and flinched as Myanna bound his ribcage. 'Whoever they were, they only wanted Amber. Otherwise they would have sent the guards down to get me too.'

Mags lay his hand on Redka's shoulder, 'It is true sire, the guards had plenty of time to retrieve Connor before we found him.'

Redka dropped down onto the bench and rested his elbows on his knees. His long white hair was secured into a braid by a tan rope, and hung over his shoulder to skim the floor.

'If anything happens to her...'

Connor exploded from the chair, knocking Myanna off balance, 'I know Redka! It wasn't my fault! We were surprised, and we will get her back.'

Redka stood up and stalked across to Connor. The two boys faced each other, their noses mere inches apart.

'Boys!' Alia entered the room and moved to stand between them, 'It is unfortunate that Amber was captured, but she is smart and powerful, and we have to put our faith in her.'

'Powerful.' Connor scoffed, 'She's blown up more rocks than a demolition team. How is that going to help her?'

'With any luck she'll blow a hole in the side of the castle and escape,' Myanna added with a hint of a smile.

Redka threw his hands in the air and turned to the group, 'You are her family and friends, and yet you mock her powers instead of helping her. She has tried to master her emotions so that she can be of service to our realm. A realm that means nothing to her, and yet here she is, helping us.'

'We are sorry Redka. We didn't mean to offend.' Alia spoke softly as she tried to calm her son.

'Offend! You have offended her most, mother. You and Myanna insist on keeping us apart, and yet we both feel stronger when we are together.'

'It is for your safety,' she started to say, but Redka had heard enough. He threw open the door and stormed from the tree house.

Myanna watched as Alia crumpled to the nearest seat, and she rushed to her side.

'I'm okay,' she said patting Myanna's hand. 'He's right though isn't he? None of us have helped Amber.'

'I've been teaching her about magic and herbs, but that's as much as I can show her. She doesn't want to listen to me, and I can't say I blame her,' said Myanna.

'The oracles are guiding her,' Connor said in a low whisper.

Myanna looked up at Connor, 'Did I hear you right? Did you say the oracles are guiding her?'

Connor nodded, 'She told me she had met the four oracles, and they had gifted her with their powers. Stealth, glamour, and strength. She was still figuring out how to use them, but I think Lavanya was helping.'

Myanna squeezed the bridge of her nose between her thumb and forefinger, 'I've failed my little girl haven't I? Instead of listening to her when she tried to talk to me, I pushed her away, and now it might be too late.'

'It's not too late,' snapped Conner, throwing his cold compress on the table and snatching up his sword, 'We'll go back tonight and get her back. Mags, can you round up your team? We leave at nightfall.'

THE FLOOR was cold against her cheek when Amber finally opened her eyes. She was lying face down on the damp flagstones, a bowl of water and a chunk of bread by her side. As she moved her head, a nauseous feeling washed over her. The rag that Aaron had used to drug her was discarded on the cell floor.

She dragged herself up to a sitting position and waited for her eyesight to adjust to the gloomy interior of the dungeon.

She was in a cage; three sides were made of reinforced metal, and the back wall appeared to be part of the outer castle wall. The adjoining cages were empty, but she could make out a mound of cloth in the shape of a body in one of the cages across the short walkway.

'Hello, can you hear me?' She shuffled to the metal cage door and held on to the bars to lift herself up. There was a flash, and she was thrown to the other side of the cage, landing heavily against the stone wall.

'What the hell!' She shook her fingers as the pain subsided in her hand.

'The cages are bound by dark magic.' A soft voice carried across from the dark corner. 'You can't use your magic here without causing yourself great pain.'

'Who are you?' Amber stayed back from the metal and squinted into the shadows.

'My name is Ninette. I am from the Great Sea.'

'You're the water sprite aren't you?'

There was a long silence before the soft voice replied, 'I *was* a water sprite. Now I fear I am an empty shell.'

'Did Nikita take your powers?'

'Her necromancer used very dark magic to extract my power from me. I could feel it being ripped out of my body, like my soul was being flayed.'

Amber wrapped her arms around her legs and rested her chin on her knees, 'I'm so sorry. I wish I could have stopped her before she hurt you.'

'How could you stop such a creature? You are just a child.'

'I'm an oracle,' said Amber, feeling a bubbling sense of pride in the pit of her stomach as she said it out loud, 'I have many powers, and many friends who will defeat Nikita and her evil necromancer.'

'Not if I ground you first young lady.'

Amber sat up straight at the sound of a new voice in the darkness, 'Who said that?'

The mound of cloth in the cage opposite sat up and crawled into the light. Amber could see a mop of dirty brown hair and a pale face shining in the flickering candlelight. Her eyes filled with tears as soon as he reached the edge of the bars, and lifted his gaze to look at her.

'Dad?' she whispered.

'Hello sweetheart.'

CHAPTER 5

The rescue team assembled in the centre of the village. Mags had divided the group into four clusters, each with a specific mission and the same goal—to get Amber out alive.

Connor was to lead the first team into the castle through the trap door. Redka was instructed to take point, and lead his team up to the main gate should a distraction be needed. Cass, the female fae, was leading the airborne division that would swoop into the castle grounds and extract their team if needed. Mags needed to remain at the treeline and manage his troops. They were all clear on the mission objective, but as they milled around the village discussing tactics, they failed to notice the intruder until it was too late.

Tom shouted out across the gathered crowd, his forehead covered with beads of sweat as the sword edge bit into his neck.

'Connor! Redka! Guys, I could do with a little bit of help over here.'

One by one the warriors turned towards Tom and froze.

Connor rushed forward drawing his sword and pointing it at the man who held Tom captive.

'You're Nikita's boyfriend.' he said loudly across the clearing.

The man laughed. 'I am whatever she wants me to be.'

'Where's Amber?' Redka had reached Connor's side and held his sword at arms-length. His eyes were flashing to Tom and the blade at his throat.

'Your friend is perfectly safe for now, but at first light she will be in considerable pain.'

Redka lurched forward, but Connor caught his arm and pulled him back.

'What happens at first light?'

'Queen Nikita's necromancer will begin extracting her powers. It's a painful process, very slow and dangerous. I'm sure she won't survive the ordeal, unless...'

'Unless what?'

'I can save her. I can bring her here and save her life...for a price.'

'What's your price?'

'I want Alia.'

A shocked ripple ran around the warriors, and they bunched together to form a tight barrier in front of the lord's treehouse.

'Are you mad?' Connor watched the expression on the newcomers face as he spoke, 'do you honestly think we would give up our queen for a human girl?'

Aaron laughed, 'Ah, but she's no ordinary human is she? She has the gift of elemental magic, and she's left a lasting impression on our necromancer.'

'We all have elemental magic here in Avaveil. That's nothing special and certainly not worth trading for a queen.'

'True, but I sense there is more to this human than you are telling me. Maybe I should just let Patricia do her worst?' He tightened his grip on Tom causing him to yelp.

'STOP!' The warriors parted to allow Queen Alia passage, her iridescent wings spread wide. She came to a halt and stood between Connor and Redka, her eyes hard and cold as she looked from Tom's pained expression to the strong warrior before her.

'So it's true then,' Aaron released his grip on Tom and dropped his sword, kneeling on the ground, 'I had to see it for myself before I could believe it.'

Connor grabbed a rope from his pack and bound the fae warrior's hands behind his back, while Redka checked on Tom.

'Your Majesty, we were told you were dead.' Aaron kept his head bowed to the floor as he addressed Alia.

'Clearly that was a lie. My sister had other plans, and my rescue was not a part of that. Have you served her long?'

'No, your Majesty. Nikita does not associate herself with the fae people, but I am a half-breed; part fae, part necromancer. This pleased her, and I was allowed to live and work in the castle.'

'Capturing and torturing young girls is one of your jobs I take it?' Tom snapped at him as he rubbed his neck.

'I didn't capture your friend. That was Patricia. I was instructed to lock her in the dungeon until first light, but then she mentioned that Queen Alia was in Avaveil and was going to take back the throne. I thought it was nonsense until I saw the power this girl possessed.'

'What did she do?'

'I fear she has scarred Patricia for life with a very well-directed fireball.'

'Ha! So much for blowing up the castle,' said Tom.

'We still have to get her out.' Connor stood before Alia and pointed at Aaron, who was now bound by hands and feet on the forest floor, 'We can't trust what he says, but it's not long until first light and I don't want to risk it.'

'Agreed. Mags, please go ahead as planned. It's imperative that we save her before my sister can do any more harm.'

Mags nodded and rallied the warriors. They melted into the forest silently, leaving a small guard to watch over Aaron.

'What are you going to do with him?' asked Tom.

'I want to have a long talk with our guest,' Alia gestured for the guard, 'Bring him up to the lord's house.'

THROUGH A veil of tears, Amber watched her father try to sit up straight. His arms were bruised, and there were ragged scars on his wrists. The right side of his gaunt face was swollen, and his bloodshot eyes seemed to sink into his skull.

'What are you doing here? You left me a note to say you'd gone on a mini-break.'

Alan laughed, but the action caused him to wince. Bending over double, he clutched his chest.

'Sorry,' he said, 'If I move or laugh, my latest wound re-opens.' He pulled his shirt aside to reveal a long deep scar that ran from just below his collar bone and down to his belly button.

'I felt that,' Amber whispered, remembering how Isha had experienced the same wound as she had. 'I met the oracles and they told me how we were linked. I feel what you feel.' She lay her hand on her belly as she spoke.

'How have you met the oracles? You never showed any signs of being the last oracle when you were a child. Your mum and I thought the prophecy had been wrong.'

'It's a long story,' Amber began, 'It started when Tom was kidnapped by supernatural soldiers and dragged to a dimension of hell. I went to save him with Connor's help, and met a fae queen and mum and then...'

He lurched forward narrowly missing the bars of the cage to interrupt her, 'Is your mother alive?'

Amber nodded as fresh tears coursed down her cheeks. Her father's face shone with the first glimmer of hope she'd seen in ten years. 'She was being held captive in Phelan. A Guardian General took her from us all those years ago. She's here in Avaveil.'

Alan wept freely. His head hung low and his scrawny shoulders shook. Amber yearned to hug him and tell him that everything was going to be okay, but as she glanced around at her surroundings she wasn't so sure that it was.

'She was being held prisoner with Queen Alia. When Connor and I reached Phelan to save Tom, we found them. I was so worried because I didn't see you before we left, and then I found your note, and I guess...well, I thought you wouldn't care what happened to me.' She dropped her head in shame. Clearly, her father had been preoccupied with his tale of terror to worry about her quest.

'I'm so sorry Amber, I don't remember leaving you a note. In fact, I don't remember much of anything from the last few years. My head always felt so foggy, and you were pulling away or growing up, or whatever teenagers do these days.' He huffed a little laugh, 'I haven't been much of a dad lately.'

'Of course you have. It's my fault dad, and I've been a terrible daughter. A proper girlie teen monster.'

Alan chuckled, 'Shall we call a truce?'

Amber laughed, 'I'd like that. When we get out of this place, we'll do all the family things we used to do with mum. We've got ten years' worth of picnics to catch up on.'

The heavy oak door at the end of the dungeon slammed opened, and Nikita breezed in, followed by her guards.

'How touching,' she purred, 'Daddy and daughter reunited for the briefest of moments.'

The guard unlocked Alan's cage and dragged him to his feet. He swayed before losing his footing and landing heavily on his knees.

'Where are you taking him?' Amber shouted through the bars, her hands tingling as her rage intensified.

'Don't worry my dear. Your daddy and I are becoming the best of friends.' She ran a silver fingernail along the metal bars in front of Amber's face. A shower of sparks rained over her as Nikita walked back and forth. 'I've taken all the magic he possesses, so he is no threat to me, but I find him intriguing for a human.' She winked at Amber and sashayed towards the door with Alan and the guards trailing behind her.

'No! Please don't take my dad.'

Alan's anguished expression was the last thing she saw as he was pulled through the doorway and whisked away from her yet again.

'LET ME see if I understand you correctly. My sister is using necromancer magic to extract the powers from the realm leaders?' She looked over at Myanna, who stood by the fire listening to the conversation. Myanna raised an eyebrow to show her distrust for what the faerie warrior said.

Aaron knelt on the wooden floor in the centre of the lord's living room. His hands and legs remained tightly bound as Alia circled him peppering him with questions.

'Yes, my queen. It began with Xavier, the leader of the orc rebellion. He tried to cheat Nikita out of lands and jewels, but her followers are loyal, and they turned on Xavier. Once captured, she called for her necromancer, a female known for her unorthodox methods amongst the residents of the Lost Lands. She took a human name and was living in the human realm, working on a specific spell of extraction on a witch's family. At Nikita's request, she returned to Avaveil and used her skills to rip the orc's power from him.'

'What happened to Xavier?'

'He died, my queen. The extraction procedure was not perfected, but Nikita was impatient. She told the necromancer to return to the human realm and complete her spell on the witch before bringing him here to study.'

'Does this witch still live?'

'Yes, my queen. The spell on the witch was a masterpiece. She had worked with this man for many years, slowly feeding off his exceptional power. When she understood how to perform the extraction without killing the host, she returned to Avaveil. So far, she has successfully removed the full powers of the witch, and the water sprite from the Great Sea.'

Alia paced back and forth as she processed this new information. Her sister's cruelty was vast, but what she needed to know was how Nikita was able to use these stolen powers.

'Once the power has been released from the host, how does this necromancer grant my sister with these gifts?'

'The essence of each great leader is injected into Nikita's blood. The necromancer mixes the energy with a binding agent and feeds it through a tube. I believe she learned this art of bloodletting from a general, who lives in the demon lands.'

Alia and Myanna gasped in unison.

'That general is dead,' said Alia, 'So when did she acquire these skills?'

'A long time ago. She traded the General's knowledge for the whereabouts of a witch he was in need of.'

Myanna gripped the ledge of the fireplace and tried to steady her breathing. 'Tell me, Aaron, what is the name of the witch that your necromancer friend has stripped of all power?'

'He is called Alan ma'am.'

Myanna sank to the floor with a cry.

'What is it Myanna? What's wrong?' Alia rushed to her friend's side.

'Alan is my husband. If what Aaron says is true, then this necromancer is responsible for ripping my family apart ten years ago, and continuing to harm them.'

Aaron chuckled from his position on the floor. 'I can understand now why Amber was so quick to attack Patricia.'

'What of Amber?' Alia stood over Aaron, her eyes as hard as flint, 'What does this necromancer want with her?'

'I believe it is her intention to extract her witch power, just like her father's was taken from him.'

'Witch power!' Myanna gathered her skirts and rose up from the floor, 'You and your necromancer have no idea what Amber is capable of.'

'Myanna!' Alia warned her to be silent.

Aaron appraised the two women. 'If I may be so bold my queen,' he said, 'I surrendered my sword as soon as I knew that you were indeed safe and well. I have answered all your questions and given you no cause to doubt me. I can help save Amber, but I need you to trust me, and I need you to release me. I am your loyal servant, but I am also Nikita's confidante, and I can get close to her and your friends. If you let me return to the castle, I can lead Amber out safely within the hour.'

Alia stared at him for a long time, until eventually she turned to the guard, 'Release him.'

'No! Alia you can't be serious.' Myanna grabbed for Alia's arm, and spun her around so they were facing each other. 'We can't trust that he won't tell Nikita where we are, and kill Amber and Alan.'

Aaron rubbed at his wrists where the guard had untied the rope. 'I understand your trepidation ma'am, but please believe me when I say I am Queen Alia's servant. I always have been, even when I lost my way. If it pleases your Majesty, then have me followed, but do not doubt that I am on your side.' He bowed his head curtly, strode to the treehouse door, and without a second glance departed.

Alia summoned the guard at the door. A young female warrior called Heidi approached.

'Fly to Redka, tell him that I have released Aaron, and he is going to free Amber. Tell him that this is my command. He must honour my decision and aid Aaron in any way needed.'

Heidi nodded and took to the sky, like a bullet from a gun, leaving Alia and Myanna alone in the lord's living room.

Myanna shuffled towards the door. As she reached the opening, she looked up at Alia with tears in her eyes. 'I hope for all our sakes that you haven't just condemned us all to death.'

CHAPTER 6

What's the holdup?' Connor was getting impatient as he waited along the dirt road for Mags to give the order to advance.

'Looks like a messenger. Isn't that Heidi from the village?' Tom strained to see the two faeries through the undergrowth. 'Mags doesn't look very happy.'

As Heidi launched herself back into the night sky, Mags made his way back along the line of warriors until he reached Redka, Connor, and Tom.

'What is it?' Redka asked.

'Queen Alia has released Aaron, and he is on his way here. Apparently, he has convinced our queen that he can help Amber to escape unharmed.'

'What a crock of shit!' Connor threw his arms up and began pacing, 'He could bring the entire minotaur army pouring through those gates and massacre the lot of us.'

'But I won't.' Aaron stepped out from behind the trees and walked straight up to the assembled group, 'I made a promise to Queen Alia, and I intend to keep it. Give me one hour.'

Redka moved forward to stand nose to nose with Aaron. They were the same height and build, but Redka was much younger than the seasoned warrior. At this proximity, Redka could see a faint tattoo running along Aaron's neck and beneath his tunic. The intricate pattern of interwoven serpents that covered a large portion of his skin was a necromancer's brand.

Redka spoke through gritted teeth, 'If you don't appear from those gates within the hour, I will personally hunt you down and drive my sword in your chest.'

Aaron bowed deeply, and then jumped down from the wooded area onto the road. He landed gracefully, and turned to salute the group that watched him with disdain. 'An hour.' Then he was gone.

AMBER DIDN'T move from her position close to the bars. She had a good view of the main dungeon door, and wanted to be alert for when they returned her father to his cell.

Ninette was good company, and tried to keep Amber's troubled mind occupied with stories of the Great Sea.

'Maybe before you return to the human realm, you will have the opportunity to visit my home,' she said softly.

'I'd like that, and I hope you'll be able to show me around.'

'I fear that my time will soon come to an end. Nikita has what she wants, so I am of no further use. I don't understand why I am still being kept captive.'

'Just how long have you been here, Ninette?'

'Twelve moons, give or take.'

'Twelve moons? You mean months? She's kept you here for a year?'

'It must be. I know she withdrew my powers at least four moons ago.'

The door to the dungeon opened quickly, and a figure dressed in black slipped in and closed it behind them. Their features were hidden from view by a heavy cloak and hood.

Amber stood up in her cell and studied the newcomer.

'Are you here to torture us or feed us?' she asked.

'Neither,' Aaron dropped his hood to reveal his trademark long white hair. 'I have come to rescue you.'

Amber stepped back from the cage wall, and squatted down into a crouching position. If Aaron was about to unlock the cell door, then she was going to be ready for him.

'Rescue me? What's with the sudden change of heart, Aaron of Avaveil?'

'I met Queen Alia. When I saw for myself that she was alive, I pledged my loyalty to her.'

'Won't your girlfriend have something to say about that?' Amber was trying to put the pieces together. If he had found Alia, then did that mean they were also imprisoned, or worse—dead? 'I'm sure Nikita won't be happy that you've chosen her sister over her. She gives off that psycho girlfriend vibe, and you shouldn't mess with that.'

'I give you no reason to trust me, but I have promised your friends that within the hour you will appear at the castle gates. They are waiting for you at the treeline.'

Amber stood up and crossed her arms. 'I don't get it. Why are you helping me, when just a couple of hours ago you were the one to throw me into this cage?'

'I am a half-breed. Part fae and part necromancer. Throughout my entire life I have been treated like a freak, ridiculed, and beaten. I was branded as a necromancer by my brothers. They hated that our mother had consorted with the scum of the realms. There was only one person who made me feel whole; one person who inspired me to join the faerie warriors many years ago and fight for a worthwhile cause. Alia.'

Amber watched Aaron's face as he recounted his story. His expression was genuine, and as he spoke she could sense the passion in his words.

'When Alia disappeared and could not be found, the warriors disbanded. Nikita killed many of them, including my family. The rest scattered, but she found me intriguing. She hated the fae with a loathing that I could relate to. She took me in, and here I stayed. Not out of love or honour, but out of a desperate need to belong. I wanted revenge.'

Amber was stunned. How could this evil warrior, who beat horses and slapped girls across the face, be so similar to her? She understood that need to belong. It was why she was in Avaveil. She had followed the dream of a reunited family and a better time.

'Okay, Aaron,' she remained wary as she moved towards the cage door, 'unlock the cage and let's have a proper chat, face-to-face.'

'Do you promise not to set me alight like you did with Patricia?'

'I can promise I'll *try* not to. I normally can't control it so well.'

Aaron chuckled, 'You looked to be in perfect control when you threw that fireball at Patricia.' He unlocked the cage and stepped back.

Amber cautiously walked through the open door and stood in between Aaron and the main dungeon exit.

'Ninette comes too,' she said, pointing at the water sprite who lay curled up on the floor.

'I can't...' Aaron began to protest, but Amber held up a hand to stop him.

'Ninette comes too, or I'm going to scream my lungs off and attract every guard in the castle.'

Aaron mumbled something under his breath as he turned the metal key in the lock and swung open the cage. Ninette's tiny frame only came up to the keyhole as she stood on shaky legs in the opening.

'What now?' Amber asked.

'Before we can leave, I need to ask for one thing. I need you to allow me to take a small portion of your power.'

'What! I knew it, this is a trick.' Amber began to back away, but Aaron held his hands up.

'No, please Amber, this is no trick. I will need you to use my dagger on me. We need to make this look like you escaped on your own. The only way I can think to make this work is if I tell Nikita I was starting to extract your power when you attacked me.'

Ninette shuffled to Amber's side and grasped her hand. 'Give over a small part of your elemental magic. Something you won't miss. Can you change the colour of a flower?'

Amber looked down into Ninette's wide blue eyes. She could almost see the Great Sea reflected in them. What small part of her magic could she afford to lose?

'I know what I can give you.' She rolled up her sleeve and took a seat on the nearest bench, 'Let's get this over with.'

AN HOUR later, Amber and Ninette emerged from the main gate. The two minotaur guards had been relieved of duty, but their replacements had been conveniently held up by a commotion in the dungeon. The girls hurried down the winding path and towards the cover of the waiting forest.

Redka, Connor, and Tom were waiting for them when they arrived. Amber rushed into Redka's arms, as Tom called for Cass to assist him in finding a blanket for the water sprite.

'Are you okay?' Redka swept his hands over Amber's face and ran his fingers through her hair, 'I was so worried about you.'

'I'm fine, honestly. I'm tougher than I look.' She turned towards Connor, 'How are you doing? That was one hell of a fall you took.'

Connor rubbed his head and gave her a lopsided smile, 'I'm tougher than I look, too.'

Amber laughed and laced her fingers with Redka's. 'Let's get out of here before Nikita finds out what I did to her boyfriend.'

'What *did* you do to Aaron?'

'I only did what I was told.' She smiled to herself as they moved off as one through the trees.

NIKITA CRASHED through the open door to the dungeon and took in the scene before her. The cages stood empty, both the girl and the water sprite were missing. A minotaur guard lay prone in the centre of the room with a large sword protruding from his back. What startled her more was the sight of Aaron splayed across the benches with a dagger in his side and a bloody face.

'What happened?' Nikita roared.

'My queen, it was all my fault,' Aaron said as he mopped the blood from his face and tried to sit up, 'The girl appeared to be under the influence of the sleeping drug, but she tricked me. I was starting the extraction when she hit me with a chunk of rock. Before I knew what had happened, she thrust my dagger into my side and fled with the sprite.'

Nikita looked around the room slowly before settling her cold, dark eyes on Aaron.

'Just why were *you* doing the extraction?'

'Patricia has been working tirelessly with the dragon, and we didn't want to delay her work, so I took it upon myself to...'

'You took it upon yourself.' She walked over to where Aaron was seated on the floor and knelt down so she was level with him. Raising her hand she slapped it hard across his face. 'We do not take it upon ourselves to do anything without my say so, do you understand Aaron?'

'Yes, my queen.' He bowed his head.

'I will send the guards into the forest and flush her out, she can't have gone far.'

'My queen, before you do, I must show you something.' He held out his clenched fist and uncurled his fingers to reveal a cluster of diamonds.

'What is this?'

'Before the girl could surprise me, I was able to extract a small portion of her elemental magic. It's nothing we've seen in the faerie realm before. It's the ability to turn tears into diamonds.'

Nikita's eyes lit up as she scooped the jewels out of Aaron's palm and studied them.

'You managed to extract this gift?'

'Yes, my queen.'

Nikita smiled down at Aaron and ran a single finger along his jaw line. 'You may not have totally failed me after all.' She stuffed the diamonds into the pocket of her dress and sauntered towards the door.

'Get this mess cleaned up!' she shouted at the minotaurs as she left the room.

Aaron exhaled slowly, and slumped back against the wall.

MYANNA ENVELOPED Amber in a warm embrace as they filed into the lord's treehouse, 'I'm so glad you're safe.'

'Mum, I'm okay. Please stop fussing over me.'

'But it could have been worse, that evil woman could have hurt you or...'

'I'm fine mum. It's not me I'm concerned about. I saw Dad, and he is in a bad way. He's covered in scars and doesn't look as if he's eaten a proper meal in weeks.'

'Your father was never given food in the cells,' Ninette said softly, 'He was always taken to Nikita's table to dine, but I don't think he ate anything when he was there.'

'Why would Nikita entertain a prisoner?'

'I think in her warped way, she's attracted to him,' Amber said, 'She mentioned that he intrigued her. Aaron said the same kind of thing and he's still alive.'

'If that's the case, it may buy us some time and keep your dad safe.'

'Buy us time for what?' asked Tom.

'If we want to rescue Alan and Roth, and at the same time overthrow Nikita, then we're going to need some help.' Connor stood in front of the group and spread a map of the realms across the table for everyone to see.

'From what Amber and I saw and heard during our brief reconnaissance, then Roth is being drugged to keep him quiet. To free a dragon, we're going to need a dragon's help. We must send a team to the dragon realm on a recruitment mission. While that team is away, the rest of us can spread word across Avaveil that Alia has returned and is here to claim her throne.'

'Do you think the fae will help?' Amber asked.

Mags and Cass both stepped forward in unison. Mags bowed his head to Alia and addressed the crowded room. 'Our people have dreamt for many years of the day our queen would return, so I volunteer to recruit the fae. I know that many will join us.'

'I volunteer to journey to the dragon realm,' Cass said, 'I can take a small team and be back in under a week.'

Tom stood up from his secluded spot at the back of the room, 'I volunteer to go with Cass.'

'Good, that's wonderful. Let's work out the details and meet back here tomorrow morning.' Connor and Mags left the treehouse with their heads drawn together in deep discussion, as Tom made his way over to Amber.

'Dragon realm?' Amber said, bumping her shoulder into his.

'It felt right like I needed a quest,' Tom said, pressing his hand over his heart.

'Nothing to do with a gorgeous faerie warrior called Cass then?'

He blushed and playfully slapped Amber's arm, 'I don't know what you mean.'

Amber laughed and threw her arm around his shoulder, 'Just promise me you'll be careful. I don't want to have to take on any more scary soldiers to save your skin.'

He gave her a quick kiss on the cheek, 'I promise cutie.' He got up and left, walking out with Cass by his side.

Redka approached and crouched beside her to whisper in her ear, 'I have to go, but can we meet later at the willow house?'

She nodded and tried not to look guilty, as Alia and Myanna watched from the other side of the room. Redka leaned forward and kissed the top of her head before leaving.

Alia rolled her eyes and said something to Myanna, but Amber didn't stay to find out what it was. She had work to do. She needed to speak to the oracles and find out just how powerful she was.

CHAPTER 7

'Try to concentrate your energies on your third eye,' Lavanya said as she pressed a delicate finger to Amber's forehead. 'Here. Concentrate on this point. This is the centre of your intuition. The point where your emotional wisdom lies. If you master this chakra point, then you master your emotions.'

Amber had been concentrating on the space between her eyebrows for an hour, and all she seemed to be able to conjure was a headache. 'Why is this so difficult?' she moaned.

'You are making it difficult because that is what you are thinking about. Change your perception, Amber, think about your final goal. Why do you want to master your emotions?'

Amber closed her eyes and thought about Lavanya's question. 'I want to stop blowing up rocks and help my friends.'

'Good, you have a purpose. What else?'

'I want to feel in control, and not be afraid of hurting anyone.'

'Excellent. Now try to picture a bright orb of violet light just in front of your eyes. Can you see it?'

Amber relaxed her body and visualised the orb. A floating blob appeared in her vision and pulsed with an indigo glow. 'I see it!' she said.

'Wonderful. Now picture more of these orbs floating outside your body. They are blue, green, yellow, orange and red. Can you see them Amber?'

She concentrated on the violet orb and saw the other colours begin to emerge with it.

They broke off one at a time and drifted down the front of her body. They looked like a rainbow as they hovered at her throat, heart and abdomen.

As she watched the floating colours, they intensified. They grew more vivid until the orbs lost their wavy edges and became strong circles of light.

She felt Lavanya close to her side and could sense her chanting as she placed her hands on the top of Amber's head.

The floating orbs exploded, and even though Amber's eyes were tightly shut, she instinctively threw her arms up to protect her face.

The colours began to whirl around her like mini cyclones, and then one by one they seeped into her body. She felt the first orb at the bottom of her spine and was filled with a sensation of strength. Her body went rigid, and her feet tingled and pulsed as if they were becoming part of the clouds she stood on.

The orange light coated her lower abdomen and left her feeling warm and safe. Her shoulders relaxed and straightened as the yellow orb filled her diaphragm. A sense of peace washed over her as her heart was engulfed in a green haze. As the light blue orb coated her throat, she coughed and could hear Lavanya chuckle from her position just behind her.

Finally, the violet orb pulsed and danced before her face and then it disappeared as if she had drawn it into her eyes. Her mind felt foggy for a moment but then cleared, leaving a strong sense of being where she was meant to be.

As she opened her eyes, she noticed that her entire body glowed purple. Lavanya finished chanting and disconnected her hands from Amber's head. 'You are ready,' she said.

'I'm purple!' Amber cried.

Lavanya laughed and stroked Amber's face. 'Only briefly, the colour will settle soon enough and you will be better equipped to feel your powers and use them accordingly.'

'How exactly do I use them?'

'You need to practise your connections. Work with the elemental magic you possess and link this with your oracle gifts. If you want to heal, then concentrate on the energy around your heart. If you need to protect yourself,

then visualise the red energy at the base of your spine and pull your power from the earth.'

Amber nodded, but her brow stayed furrowed, 'Don't get me wrong. I understand that this is who I am now, but it's going to take some getting used to.'

'I know, little eye. Just embrace it and be confident in your abilities. You truly are a powerful young woman, and once you build your knowledge you will fulfil your destiny.'

This was the third time someone had mentioned destiny or prophecy around her, and she had tried to figure out what it meant. As if sensing her questions, Lavanya held up a slim hand.

'Your destiny can wait, little eye. All in good time. Now you must return to Avaveil as I believe your prince awaits.'

AMBER'S EYES fluttered open to see Redka propped up on his elbow next to her.

'Hello, sleepyhead,' he bent forward and kissed her tenderly on the lips, 'I wondered if you were ever going to wake up.'

'Sorry, I was in the oracle realm, and I guess I lost track of time. Or maybe there is no time in the clouds. Oh, I don't know, but I'm here now and very happy to wake up to see your face.'

They kissed again and this time it was deeper and longer. Redka lay back on the blanket and pulled Amber closer as he swept his hands along her ribcage. Her body tingled as it responded to his touch. She rested her hand on the tight muscles of his chest, feeling his heartbeat beneath his tunic. All too soon he pulled away. 'Amber,' he whispered, breathlessly. His face flushed. 'I love you.'

She smiled up at him and felt the vibration around her heart. Her body felt heavy and warm all of a sudden, and she had an insane urge to giggle. Is this what love felt like?

'I love you too.' It was the easiest sentence she had ever spoken, and she knew it was true.

They languished in their willow house for a long time, talking over the events of their recent adventures, and the possibilities open to the fae folk should Avaveil be restored to its former glory.

'Amber, can I ask you something?'

'Of course,' she said, her head resting on his chest as she listened to him breathe.

'How long have your eyes been purple?'

She sat bolt upright and blinked. 'What?'

'Your eyes are purple, like a faerie.'

'Ohmigod I'm going to kill Lavanya.'

Redka laughed and pulled her back down on the blanket. He hovered over her and stared into her eyes. 'They suit you.'

She swatted at his arm and laughed, 'At least they're purple and not luminous yellow or something. I should be grateful for that I suppose.'

Redka jumped up off the blanket and held out a hand to Amber, 'Come on my faerie princess, we have work to do.'

She reluctantly took his hand, and allowed herself to be dragged from her comfy position on the floor of their willow house.

'What do you have in mind?' she asked.

'Cass and Tom left for the dragon realm this morning, so we have about four days to help you master your powers before they return. From what you told me, Lavanya has opened up your energy channels and now all we have to do is fine tune them.'

'Oh, that's *all* we have to do. What if Alia's vision is right and during our fine tuning, I blow up a tree and it squashes you?'

'I shall take my chances.' He looked around at the mighty oak and sweet chestnut trees that surrounded the clearing outside their willow house. 'Maybe I could wear a hat or something,' he teased her as she threw a handful of fallen leaves at him.

They chased one another around the clearing until collapsing in a giggling heap on the floor. 'We must get to work Amber,' said Redka between breathless laughs.

She kissed his lips briefly, 'I'm ready. Let's do this.'

They found a spot on the moss-covered forest floor to sit cross-legged and face each other. Redka instructed her to relax her posture and take a deep breath. 'Place your hands on the ground and connect to the energy of nature.'

Amber obeyed and spread her palms wide on the floor. She could feel the moss tickling her fingers and the gritty sensation of the soil beneath her fingertips.

Redka continued, 'Imagine a bubble of protection around us; a clear, clean bubble with just the two of us inside.'

As he spoke the word 'protection', she felt her body fill with the red energy that Lavanya had told her about. She pulled an imaginary circle from the ground that surrounded them. Then she lifted a veil of shimmering air up and over the top of them, like they were sitting inside a snow globe. The red energy subsided, and the bubble filled with a bright white light.

'Done it,' she said, keeping her eyes closed.

'Good. Now I want you to feel with your energy to the outside of our protection bubble, and move the fallen leaves.'

Amber concentrated, and Redka watched as a few leaves leapt into the air and fluttered back down to earth.

'Excellent, keep trying. Connect your gifts from the oracles.'

'What if something terrible happens?'

'It won't, Amber. I believe in you.'

She smiled as a deep sense of calm crept over her. 'Isn't it cheating if you use your faerie calming magic on me?'

'I'm not, you're doing it all yourself.'

She opened her eyes to look down, and realised that they weren't touching. Redka sat a short distance from her, silhouetted by a curtain of silver that shone all the way around them. The stillness she felt was coming from somewhere deep inside her.

She glanced to the right of Redka and saw Diva's image, like a ghostly spectre, floating outside the circle. The oracle was smiling, and as Amber watched her, a silver fog descended over them to coat their protective bubble.

Amber glanced down at her hands, as they began to change form. Her fingers lengthened and dug into the soil, turning into tree roots. The deeply grooved bark wound its way up to her elbows. She could feel the trees around them; like a heartbeat vibrating through the forest.

Concentrating on the fallen leaves, they lifted from the forest floor and whirled around the clearing, spinning and dancing. They chased each other around the protection bubble as Amber laughed, and Redka's mouth hung open.

'I can feel them,' she said, 'I can feel the leaves, and the soil, and the moss.'

'You are using your glamour gift, and working with it to enhance your elemental magic.'

He watched as the leaves danced around them, and then settled his gaze on Amber. 'You are the most beautiful person I have ever known, Amber Noble.'

Amber's heart lurched in her chest as she disconnected from the glamour. Her hands returned to normal, and the forest grew quiet once more. She leaned forward and kissed him, winding her hands around his neck and pulling him close.

'Thank you,' she whispered between kisses.

Redka buried his face in her neck and dusted her with tender little kisses, moving up along her jaw line. 'Stay with me in Avaveil, Amber. Promise you will stay with me forever.'

Amber tensed in his arms. 'I can't make you that promise.' She moved back to sit opposite him and her heart broke at the pain she saw in his face. 'I've been reunited with my mother, and when my father is safe I will have my family back together. I need to keep them safe, and return Tom and Connor to Hills Heath.'

'They don't want to leave.'

She thought back briefly to one of the conversations she had with Tom. He had told her how much he loved this place, how he felt at home in the woodland village. Connor felt the same, and he had grown in strength and character since arriving in the faerie realm. Even she was a different person than a few weeks ago. But the facts were simple; Avaveil wasn't her home. She shook her head, 'I can't make that promise, Redka, I'm sorry.'

Standing up, she dusted off her trousers, 'I think I better get back to the village before Myanna sends out a search party.'

Redka looked so sad that she couldn't bear to look at him. She walked into the forest without glancing back.

CHAPTER 8

The giant urn smashed against the castle wall as Nikita launched it at Patricia. The quivering necromancer just managed to step out of its path. Shards of tan-coloured pottery showered over her as she flinched away from the explosion.

'You told me I would have the dragon's power by the end of the day. I want that power.' Nikita rose from her chair and stormed towards Patricia. She circled her fingers around the necromancer's neck and lifted her off the floor.

Patricia clawed at Nikita's arms. 'Please, your Majesty, the dragon power is more difficult to extract than we anticipated. I just need more time.'

Nikita glowered at Patricia as she squirmed in her grasp. She squeezed her hand tighter, pleased to see the panicked expression on Patricia's face. 'I need that power. The orc and the water sprite were weak and their powers have been spent. I want the dragon's strength.'

Patricia tried in vain to prise Nikita's fingers from her throat. 'I understand, my queen. None of us expected the powers that we extracted to wear off. We just assumed that once they were taken, and then transferred into your blood stream, that they would be permanent.'

'You were wrong,' Nikita hissed. Her top lip curled back in a snarl, as she flung the necromancer to the side where she landed heavily amongst the shards of broken pottery.

She settled herself down on the plush throne at the end of the room. The creamy stone seat was covered in throws and cushions from far off realms, all hand-spun from the finest silks. Nikita played with the frayed edge of a deep purple blanket as she studied the crumpled necromancer.

'Aaron extracted a very unusual power from the witch's girl. The very same girl whom you spent the last ten years living with. Why did you not tell me of her gift?'

Patricia crawled on her knees until she was at Nikita's feet. 'Majesty, I had no idea of the girl's power. She was just a brat, and a hindrance to my extraction spell on Alan. She became more tiresome as the years passed, and I was certain that raising the demon to kill her friend would break the child. I had no idea she had inherited her father's talents.'

Nikita laughed; the sound echoing off the cold walls. 'She inherited more than you could imagine, my dear necromancer.'

She clapped her hands, and two guards burst through the doors carrying Alan Noble between them. His tattered trousers and stained shirt hung from his thin frame, as he was unceremoniously dumped on the floor at Nikita's feet.

'My sweet Alan, how frail you look.' She stood and walked over to where he lay in a heap on the floor. Her long black skirt brushed his face, while she circled around him like a vulture surveys its meal. He closed his eyes and lay his head on the flagstones.

'Come now Alan, this is no time for a nap. I want to have a little chat.' Kneeling down next to him she scooped his chin in her hand and lifted his head. 'Tell us about your sweet Amber.'

Alan flinched away from Nikita's touch and pushed himself into a sitting position.

'Stay away from my daughter, both of you.' He swung around to look at Patricia, his expression one of loathing.

'Now why would we want to do that when the girl can turn tears into diamonds?'

'You're lying.'

'Oh, no, my love.' She scooped the diamonds from her pocket and threw them on the floor in front of Alan, 'Aaron was able to extract her gift before she beat and stabbed him and fled with my water sprite.'

Alan shook his head as he looked from the tiny jewels glistening on the floor to Nikita's cruel glare. 'It's impossible. She never showed any signs of being a witch when she was growing up.'

Nikita laughed in an over-exaggerated fashion as she returned to sit on her throne. 'A witch! Do you honestly expect me to believe that she is a witch?'

'What do you mean?'

'Come now, how many witches have this gift?' She looked over at Patricia as if extending her question out to her captive audience. 'I'll tell you how many witches. None.'

'Alan is right, my queen. I lived with the girl for many years, and she didn't present any magical skills at all.'

Nikita pressed the tips of her fingers together to form a pyramid with her hands and gazed up at the ceiling, deep in thought. The small space between her palms filled with a dark green orb that pulsated and oozed.

Patricia rose from her knees quickly and bowed her head low, 'Please, my queen, I beg you...'

Nikita threw the orb at the necromancer. It hit her full in the chest and knocked her the entire length of the room. She crashed into a dark oak table, smacking her head off the heavy wood. With blood pouring from the gash in her head, she stumbled to her feet. Nikita approached slowly, tossing the magical energy between her hands like a ball.

'Ten years you had this girl under your roof. Ten years you extracted the powers from this man,' she inclined her head in Alan's direction, 'When there was a stronger source within your grasp. You have failed me Patricia, and I think our time together has come to an end.'

Patricia screamed as her body was engulfed in the green fire. She writhed and bucked as the pain intensified, and her skin bubbled and charred. She stumbled backwards, falling over the leg of an upturned chair. Her piercing cry filled the air as she flung herself through the stained glass window.

Nikita stood looking through the broken glass for a long moment before turning her attention to Alan.

'Somewhere out there,' she pointed beyond the jagged remains of the window, 'is your daughter. If you don't want me to send my army out to kill her, then you *will* tell me what she is.'

Alan hung his head in defeat, 'I don't know what she is capable of,' he whispered, 'I just know the oracles guide her.'

Nikita's eyes shone in the candlelight, and her lip curled up into a menacing smile. The sharp edges of her wings shook as she clapped her hands together.

'Get me Aaron!' she shouted through the door to her guard. Within minutes, Aaron strode through the door and knelt before her.

'Go to the guardhouse and rally a group to escort you to the forest. Find Amber Noble and bring her back to me.'

'My queen, is the gift I extracted from her unstable?'

'Not at all. In fact, it appears to be the only power that hasn't evaporated. I want the girl for other reasons.'

Aaron gestured towards Alan, 'Shall I return the witch to the cells?'

'No, no. Alan stays with me until he can be reunited with his daughter. I think she may need a little gentle persuasion to hand over her oracle powers.

Aaron was startled. 'She has oracle powers?'

'My sweet love tells me that the oracles guide his little girl. Now I know for a fact that the oracles don't guide anyone unless they are a direct descendant.' She rubbed her hands together in anticipation of her greatest trophy.

'Together we will extract every ounce of power from that girl making me the most powerful being in this, and every realm. If the prophecy is true, then she can burn cities and bring about total destruction. I can wipe the faerie race from the face of the realms and rule over everything.'

'My queen, if she is so strong, then surely she will be well guarded.'

Nikita smiled and dragged a blood red fingernail down Aaron's cheek, leaving a thin scar in its wake. 'Kill anyone who gets in your way, but bring me that girl.'

Aaron bowed and walked in the direction of the door, but not before giving Alan the tiniest of nods. Alan watched his retreating back with the faintest flicker of hope burning in his chest.

TOM CLUTCHED the gateway key in his hand as they approached the entrance to the dragon realm. The journey across Avaveil had been uneventful, yet emotionally draining for the group. Fae villages had been burnt to the ground, and the dwellers were forced to take shelter in the caves and outcroppings of the mountain range that formed the edge of Avaveil.

On several occasions, the travellers had encountered sick or dying faeries. According to Cass, that was a highly uncommon situation. Time was not on their side as they trudged onwards with heavy hearts, unable to help until their mission was completed.

'We do fade and die, but only after centuries of living a full life and producing a healthy line of offspring,' Cass had told him.

Many of the stronger fae had joined their band. Each one wanted to help Queen Alia return to the throne and bring peace to the land once more.

'Are you ready?' Cass stood at Tom's side as they faced the curtain of cloud between the two realms. Only very strong magic could open the gate, or the gateway key that Amber had taken from Loso before he perished. Tom stared at the brassy ornament, which he still thought resembled a pocket watch, as the runes covering its surface began to glow. In the same way that the plush velvet curtain would pull apart to reveal a stage at a theatre, the white cloud parted allowing Tom his first glimpse of the dragon realm.

The key pulsated in his open hand as the small group walked between the billowing swathes of cloud. As they left the greenery of Avaveil behind them, the scenery shifted, and they were bathed in an indigo wash. The sky was a mixture of blues and violets, which gave the clouds floating overhead a purple coating. Beyond the clouds, the sky was a deep, dark blue, and studded with millions of stars. There were two heavy moons in the sky that shone brightly, illuminating the tall pine trees and the gigantic mountain range which dominated the skyline.

Once they had cleared the gateway, the small group stopped to take in the wonder of their surroundings. The realm was beautiful, in a mesmerising way. A loud screech filled the air to their left, and Tom spun to see a dragon soar over the mountain top. It was huge, with a dark-green leathery body, and wings that stretched out far at its side. It circled above them, its bright eyes watching them curiously. Dipping its wing, the beast dropped lower, flying over the top of their heads and whipping up a windstorm in its wake.

Tom covered his nose and mouth as he watched the dragon sweep past and return to the sky.

'He just wanted to check us out,' said Cass, resting a hand on Tom's shoulder. 'He'll tell the Dragon Keeper that we are here, and she will come to meet us.'

'Dragon Keeper? I didn't realise that someone looked after them.'

Cass laughed, 'She doesn't look after them exactly, and they are quite capable of keeping themselves safe. She just handles negotiations with other realms on their behalf.'

Tom nodded as he watched the huge dragon fly off to the north. Cass extended a finger and pointed beyond the retreating dragon. 'Can you see there, beyond the treeline, set into the side of the mountain? That is the Keeper's home?'

Tom followed the line of Cass's finger and squinted into the distance. Set into the rock of the mountain itself was a circular tower; a single structure nestled amongst the violet hue of the surrounding landscape. Its creamy colour looked out of place in the darkness of the mountain. As he watched, he could see the dragon land squarely on the rooftop and heard the low rumble of his call.

'We will set up camp here for tonight. The Keeper will join us tomorrow.' Cass barked her orders to her fellow warriors, and they set about building a camp fire and unpacking the blankets.

'Want to join me for a walk?' She winked at Tom and strode off in the direction of the pine trees. He followed, dropping his backpack and quickening his pace to catch up with her.

He pushed through the low-level pine branches and followed Cass as she edged further into the forest. The floor had a slight incline, and as they walked they gained elevation. After what felt like an hour of walking, Tom was ready to call a halt and collapse in a sweaty heap on the floor. However, just as he opened his mouth to protest to Cass, she stopped walking.

'We are here,' she said.

Tom caught up to her and bent over, resting his hands on his knees and panting as he tried to catch his breath.

'Where exactly is *here*?' he gasped.

Cass took a step to the side to allow Tom a clear view of the valley below. He slowly stood up straight, allowing his eyes to take in the whole scene before him. Enormous purple mountains surrounded a deep valley, with a large expanse of water in the centre. Majestic pine trees littered the rolling banks of the lake. To the right of the lake, on a grassy meadow, was a cluster of stone houses with thatched roofs. They were laid out in a semi-circle around a roaring fire filling the centre. Tom could see people milling around the fire and walking to and fro between the water's edge and the houses.

'What is this place?' He whispered, afraid to speak too loudly and shatter the moment. The scene looked like a painting at an exhibition; the brush strokes capturing the essence of this magical place perfectly.

'That is where I come from.' Cass smiled up at Tom with a look of pride in her face. 'I was born on this lake, and my family still lives here. When I was old enough, I joined Queen Alia's forces. When she disappeared I decided to stay put and try to help the remaining fae who were being punished by Nikita.'

'When did you last see your family?'

'The day I left to become a warrior. I made a promise to return if I could, but with the turmoil that Avaveil was in, I never got the chance.'

'So, do you think they'll be home?'

Cass grinned and nodded her head to the side, 'Let's find out shall we? Follow me.'

She shot off down a winding path that Tom hadn't seen when they arrived. The tiny path snaked down the side of the mountain, heading around to the right and towards the village.

As they drew nearer, Tom could hear laughter and singing from the people who gathered around the fire. A deep feeling of comfort and belonging seeped through him at the sound, and he quickened his pace.

THERE WERE seven stone houses in total, each one a replica of its neighbour. The thatch was trimmed neatly, and bound around large timbers that covered the stone base. Just like the Keeper's turret, the houses were a creamy colour that twinkled in the firelight.

The smell of roasting meat wafted up to greet them as they entered the village.

Cass stood with her back to the lake, and she glanced around the assembled group who were oblivious to their arrival. 'Looks like I'm just in time for supper.'

A large man in a green tunic leapt from his seat and rushed forward, drawing his sword as he moved. Tom skidded backwards, taken by surprise. He cursed himself for leaving his pack back at their camp, as it held his dagger. He looked around quickly for a make-shift weapon and stooped to grab a large jagged rock from the water's edge.

The man stopped a short distance from Cass, holding his sword to her throat. His face changed as he clearly recognised the intruder, and he dropped his sword to the ground.

'Cass!' He flung himself at the faerie, wrapping big hairy arms around her back and pulling her into a tight embrace.

'Hello, father.'

As if realising he had an audience, he released Cass and strode over to where Tom stood, brandishing his rock.

'Don't be afraid, young man.' He motioned to Tom's weapon of choice.

'Ah yes, sorry about that. I'm still getting used to being attacked, so it's a force of habit to grab the first thing I can find to defend myself.' He shrugged, cast the stone aside, and extended his hand to the big man. 'I'm Tom.' Cass's father took his hand and shook it vigorously, before pulling Tom into a tight hug.

'Any friend of our Cass, is a friend of ours,' he boomed. 'Come, join us at the fire and tell us your tales.'

CHAPTER 9

Aaron halted his band of cutthroats and thieves as they reached the western woods. Nikita's idea of a parting gift for her finest warrior was to bestow him with the worst human scum she could find. Ever since Nikita had detached herself from the fae people, and begun consorting with minotaurs and necromancers, the dregs of humanity had found their way to the realm to offer allegiance to the cruellest of queens. Murderers from the human realm had bought their passage to Avaveil from the pirates of the Great Sea, which linked their worlds. They poured through the watery gateway looking for any excuse to rape and pillage the fae folk in Nikita's name.

That Nikita assigned these men to Aaron meant she was hoping for a bloody fight, and was not expecting there to be any survivors. He purposely took them in the wrong direction, walking for miles along the empty river bed of the Veil River, winding towards the mountain region, and looping across the western tip of the realm. He had to keep them far away from the woodland village that Alia and her friends were occupying, but he knew he couldn't keep them away for much longer. Alia's base was on the main route between the castle and other neighbouring towns. These towns provided important trade for the population of Avaveil and were visited on a regular basis.

She had chosen her base well. They could stay hidden from passing trade when necessary, using the forest to screen them, or confront any threat that approached. The village was well guarded, and Aaron knew the fae warriors who lived there. They had once been a strong force within Alia's army before her disappearance. With her return came the flicker of hope that the fae folk had whispered about around their camp fires. From Aaron's perspective, as the enemy, it would eventually become a necessary place for his mercenaries to search. If he avoided the area totally, then these men would suspect something was amiss. He had to reach Alia and warn her they were coming.

'We will camp here and start out at first light,' Aaron said.

'We ain't been searching for long, can't we just keep goin'?' said a scruffy human with a long black beard.

Aaron patted the man on the back as he walked past, and uncurled the taupe on the wagon that would carry their prisoner back to the castle.

'Well, if you would rather hunt than drink, be my guest.' He leant against the barrel of wine he had taken from the castle store with a grin painted across his face, 'What our mighty Queen Nikita doesn't know won't hurt her.'

The men cheered and bustled towards the casket to retrieve a mug and have their fill.

'You're a good'un Aaron. Ain't many leaders who treat their army with such gifts.'

Aaron gave a quick nod of thanks and left the men to their wine. He needed to let them drink the entire contents for the drugs he had laced it with to work. They would sleep like the dead, and then wake with sore heads in the morning, giving Alia's warriors a fighting chance.

He settled down to watch them drink.

MYANNA AND Connor watched with open mouths as Amber lifted the fallen tree trunk with her magic, and repositioned it on the other side of the clearing. When Amber disconnected with her glamour, she was grinning from ear to ear.

'Amazing!' said Myanna, rushing over to give her a hug.

'I'm...gob smacked,' Connor said as he bumped shoulders with Amber. 'That's pretty cool. India would be so proud.'

Amber laughed out loud, 'There's no need to add to the shocked expression, you know. I have been practising.'

'Lavanya has done wonders as your guide, far better that I could have done.' Myanna smiled sheepishly at her daughter.

'Not true, mum. You've taught me so much about the healing balms, and how to channel nature to find the right cures. I'm sure that will be invaluable when we start to fight back against Nikita. And besides, when I worked with you, I didn't end up with purple eyes!'

Myanna shrugged and gathered up her bag, 'I think they look very pretty. I'll see you both back at the village for supper, okay?' She wandered off into the forest, humming a tune as she went.

'Your mum seems happier these days.'

Amber watched her mother disappear and looked over at Connor, 'She does doesn't she? I wonder why?'

Connor snorted, 'Isn't she allowed to be happy?'

'Of course she is, but it seems that ever since I told her my dad was alive and here in Avaveil, she's been humming. It's just odd because she hasn't talked about him since we found each other again. I mean, she asked after his health, but that was about it. I was starting to wonder if getting them together again was such a good idea.'

'I'm sure she's looking forward to being reunited with your dad after so long.'

'I guess, I just...,' her voice trailed off as Redka appeared in the clearing.

Connor was caught in between the two of them, and as if sensing the tension, he retrieved his sword from the ground and backed towards the treeline.

'I won't tell anyone that I saw you together,' he said as he backed away, 'Just be careful and get back to the village soon, Amber.' He looked pointedly at her and then smiled briefly at Redka before disappearing.

REDKA HELD his hands out at his sides, 'Truce?'

'No need for any truce, we didn't fall out.' She walked across the clearing, wrapped her arms around his waist, and rested her head on his chest.

He lifted her chin with his index finger and kissed her lightly on the lips.

'I don't want to fight with you, Amber. Not when there's so much more we could be doing.' He kissed her again, and she giggled against his lips.

'I'd much rather be doing this than fighting too,' she said.

His hands rested gently on her hips as he kissed her deeply, his tongue flicking across her bottom lip and sending shivers up her spine. His hands slowly moved under her blouse to touch the skin on her back, as he pressed her closer. Her body responded, and she melted against him surrendering to his kisses, and letting her hands explore the ridges of muscle on his shoulders.

Their kisses grew more passionate, until they were both breathing hard and fast. Amber wound her hands behind Redka's neck, pulling him deeper into the kiss. She could feel a cool breeze whipping around them as they stood in the clearing, locked in their embrace. There wasn't a sound from the forest, only the vibration of their two hearts beating as one.

Her hair blew around her face in a frenzy, as Redka's hand pressed against the back of her neck, holding her tighter and kissing her harder. She felt weightless and lightheaded, as if they were the only two people existing in the world. Redka pulled away gasping, his face flushed and his heart pounding. His eyes flickered briefly left, then right, before settling on Amber.

'I need you to take a deep breath and think about how soft and sturdy the forest floor is.'

She looked at him as if he was talking gibberish, 'What on earth are you talking about?'

'We're levitating, Amber.'

She flinched and looked down. The forest floor was a few feet below them, as they floated in the centre of the clearing. Amber screamed, and the two of them plummeted to the ground with a heavy bump.

Redka rolled onto his side clutching his ribs.

'Redka, are you hurt?' she shouted in a panic. When she looked more closely, she noticed he was laughing.

'I'm fine,' he said between laughs, 'No permanent damage.'

Amber lay back on the moss and exhaled loudly, 'You scared me.'

He leaned over her and looked at her shoulder blades.

'What are you doing?'

'I'm checking for wings,' he said. 'First the purple eyes, and now you take me for a flying lesson. If you're not turning into a faerie, then I'll plait sawdust.'

She thumped him playfully on the arm.

AS THEY lay side by side on the ground, the bushes parted and Aaron strode into the clearing, his face covered in a sheen of sweat as if he had been running.

Amber jumped to her feet, 'What are you doing here?' She began backing away, a sense of panic rising in her chest.

Aaron held his hands up in surrender, 'I'm not here to hurt you. I need to warn Queen Alia that I am about to attack.'

'You want to warn us that you are going to attack us?' Redka said, confused.

'Yes, Nikita has sent me to find Amber and bring her to the castle, but I am not alone. The group of men she has assigned to me are dangerous, and they will not think twice about killing every single one of you.'

'Is my father okay?'

'Yes, he is fine. I saw him yesterday. I fear that if I don't return you to the castle though, it may be Alan who suffers.'

'There is no way you are taking Amber.' Redka pushed her behind him as he gripped the hilt of his sword.

'I know. I was hoping we could work out an alternative, but first I need to warn Alia and the village of these men.'

Redka studied the warrior for a long moment. His tunic was made of black leather and looked well worn. There was a cut in the side where he had recently been wounded. His long white hair fell in wisps around his face and stopped at his shoulders. Two thin braids hung to the side and were tied together with charms attached to twine. He had seen many battles, judging by the scars on his arms. However, Redka still struggled to believe that this fae could be trusted.

'Let's take him to Alia,' Amber tugged on Redka's sleeve until he turned away from Aaron. 'She'll know what to do.'

THE VILLAGE was quiet as many of the fae folk had retired to their homes for the night. The smell of home cooking filled the air as they walked past the row of houses lining the main street. The lord's treehouse stood proudly in the centre of the village, with two guards posted on either side of the huge staircase that wound around the perimeter of the trunk.

Redka led the three of them up the wooden stairs, until they reached the circular living area at the very top of the tree.

The rotund little lord of the village was seated at the table enjoying a calming herbal tea with Alia when they entered the room. His expression darkened when he spotted Aaron. 'What is this? The queen is resting.'

Alia placed her hand on the lord's arm, 'It is quite alright. It would appear to be urgent by the expression on my son's face.'

Aaron stopped short of the door and spun to look at Redka, 'Your son!'

Redka bowed his head, but Amber pushed them forward into the room and closed the door.

'We haven't got time for the introductions,' she said, 'Aaron has news.'

Recovering quickly from his shock, Aaron recounted the tale of his mercenary army that lay drugged and sleeping not far from the village.

'They expect us to resume our search at first light. That means we will be passing this way around noon. I can scout further afield, but they will notice if I keep off this road.'

'I understand, Aaron. I owe you a great debt for delivering this message, and for honouring your word to help Amber escape.'

Aaron knelt before Alia, 'It is impossible to avoid a confrontation, my queen, but there is time enough for you and your friends to get to safety.'

'We will not run from these barbarians, Aaron. The fae of this village are ready for a fight.' She spoke to the stout lord in a hushed voice, and he hurried from the room throwing Aaron a scathing look as he passed by. 'The children will be taken to safety, but the rest of us will stand and fight. Just how many of these human fighters do you have?'

Aaron stood and approached the table where the maps of the castle and surrounding area lay open. He traced his finger along the main route through the village to a northern point just beyond the woods.

'There are twenty men, and we are camped here,' he told them, 'I left them sleeping off the after effects of a barrel of drugged wine. They shouldn't stir until dawn.'

'Impressive.' Redka walked to stand beside Aaron, a hint of admiration playing on his features. 'Won't they know what you did?'

'Not at all. They will think the wine was too rich for their human bellies, and that the aches in their head are a simple reaction to a good evening. They are not the brightest of men.'

'That's humans for you,' mumbled Redka.

'Agreed,' Aaron answered with a smile.

Amber cleared her throat from her spot by the fireplace, 'When you've quite finished... I'm human...well, I was or am, sort of.'

'Apologies,' both Redka and Aaron said at the same time.

'Oh great, another double act.' Amber threw her hands in the air and walked towards the window.

Alia chuckled and tapped the maps with a delicate finger, 'When you are quite finished upsetting our oracle, can we focus on a plan?'

The door to the room burst open, and Connor walked in with Mags close behind. He eyed Aaron warily and swept his gaze over Redka, who was bent over the maps discussing boundaries with Nikita's warrior.

'Cosy scene,' he said coldly, 'I understand you're planning to kill us all before lunch.'

Aaron stepped away from the maps and regarded Connor, 'I have come to warn you so we can work out a defensive strategy. I could turn around, return to my men, and be back to slice you open after breakfast if you prefer.'

Connor rushed forward, but Redka jumped in his path grabbing his arms and holding him back from Aaron, who stood his ground. 'He is our ally, Connor, not our enemy.'

'You've changed your tune,' he jerked his arms out of Redka's reach, 'It wasn't that long ago that this man held Amber captive.'

Redka spoke through gritted teeth, 'He aided Amber's escape, and she is safe once more. I will say this for the last time, Connor. This man is our ally, not our enemy. We will work together, or you will be asked to leave our village.'

'Redka!' Amber was stunned by his outburst, 'If Connor leaves, then I leave. We came here as a group, and we will stay together.' She turned to face Connor, 'Aaron is trying to help us, so we will play nice. Do you both understand me?' Both boys nodded their consent, as Aaron lowered his head to conceal his smile. 'Right then, let's work out our plan of attack.'

THE MEN groaned loudly as they opened their eyes to the first light of dawn. Aaron stood over them as they began to stir.

'It appears that you had a good night, my friends.'

The black-bearded man dragged himself to a sitting position and clutched his head, 'Blimey sire, that was good stuff you give us last night, but me head is poundin' like a drum.'

Aaron slapped his shoulder, 'No time for slacking, my friend. We have faeries to find. Come on, everyone up.' He walked through the men as they lay strewn across the forest floor, and kicked their legs to nudge them awake.

They stretched and coughed in the early morning air, and Aaron noted how unsteady they were on their feet.

'If you would rather return to the warmth of the castle, then I'm sure Queen Nikita will have the fires burning and hot food on the stove.'

'No sire, we'll be right in a minute. Just need to get movin' and find us a prize worthy of a queen.' He coughed and spat a chunk of chewing tobacco on the ground. 'Ain't that right lads?' The men grunted, and shuffled to collect their weapons. Aaron kept his smile hidden beneath the hood of his cloak.

'Let's move out then, gentlemen.' He strode off into the forest heading towards the main route for Alia's village. The sounds of men stumbling and moaning filled the air behind him.

They crashed through the forest for about an hour, making so much noise that every animal in the vicinity had fled the area. Aaron pushed them harder, shouting orders to move faster at every opportunity. The men were covered in a sheen of sweat, and every so often he could hear one of them vomit into the undergrowth. Two hours later they had reached the main road.

'This road leads back to the castle, but passes through one of the last villages we can search. I know the lord who resides there, and I'm sure he will let us rest for a while.'

'I ain't restin' in any faerie hole,' the black-bearded man pushed his way to the front of the group, 'We should rest up 'ere and then hit the village.'

The other men nodded their approval, as Aaron unclipped his cloak. 'Very well, rest here, and I will scout ahead.' He threw his cloak at the bearded man and melted into the trees.

'DID YOU 'ear somethin?' The human mercenaries huddled around a small fire as they fought to keep warm. Their fae captain had been gone for a while, and they were eager to get moving again. 'Came from over there.' The man pointed a dirty fingernail in the direction of a thick cluster of oak trees. The trunks were huge, and the branches were heavy with leaves that swept low over the forest.

Before he could say another word, an arrow struck him in the chest, throwing his body backwards and into another man who leapt to his feet yelling.

There was chaos as the humans jumped for their weapons and swung their swords at an invisible enemy. One by one, they were picked off by arrows. The men scattered, charging for the treeline with their swords above their heads.

Connor and Mags dropped from the trees as two of the mercenaries ran beneath them. Taking them by surprise they ran them through with their swords.

Mags gestured for Connor to veer to the left, as he swung to the right, cutting down a small, wiry man as he went.

Connor could hear the cries of the men and the whistle of the arrows as they found their targets all around him. He rushed through the trees towards Redka, who was making sure none of the men made it beyond the edge of the village. If anyone slipped through, then Myanna and Amber were positioned on the village outskirts. Alia had been removed from sight and kept under guard in the treehouse. Everything was in place for a swift victory.

The fae warriors were relentless with their onslaught. They took out all the rage they carried for Nikita on the human scum that invaded their land. Screams filled the air as Connor reached Redka's side.

'Everything is going to plan,' he said.

Redka notched another arrow in his bow and let it loose, as a tall man with grey hair barrelled towards them. The man flew backwards as the arrow buried itself in his chest, the impact knocking him off his feet. He was dead before he hit the ground. Redka quickly readied another arrow.

'We should make our way back to the village,' he said, 'I think we have killed the majority of these barbarians, but we need to ensure there are no stragglers.'

The two boys headed for the road, whistling to their fellow fae to fall back.

Once on the road, they regrouped. Only one of them had been injured. A young fae called Jana had been stabbed in her side, and blood poured from the wound as two of her friends helped her.

Redka appraised the injury, 'Take her immediately to the tree-house. My mother will be able to help her.'

The two female warriors scooped Jana up between them, and launched into the air to return to the village. Connor quickly took a head count of who was left. Four male fae warriors stood guard at the treeline, and three female warriors flanked Redka and himself.

'We need to get back to Amber and make sure the boundary wasn't breached,' Connor directed.

They moved silently along the road, listening for sounds of any remaining men who were stumbling around blindly in the forest. Before long, they arrived at the ridge where the road widened before the approach into the village.

Redka whistled long and low, until Amber emerged from her hiding spot in a large chestnut tree. She dropped gracefully to the ground and helped Myanna climb down the branches.

'Is it over?' she asked the boys.

'Aaron will need to confirm the numbers for us when he returns, but I think we got them all.' Amber wrapped her arms around Redka and hugged him. They all began to move off towards the village, while Myanna rushed back to collect the bag of herbs she had hidden at the base of the tree trunk.

'Was anyone hurt?' Myanna called to them.

'Jana was injured. She's been taken back to Queen Alia at the village,' Connor said over his shoulder.

'I must get back to them in case she needs me. Redka, shall I tell your mother that it's safe?'

Before she could say anything else, a sharp blade bit into her neck. Dirty hands enveloped her, and dragged her to a sudden stop. She cried out.

The group spun around to see a filthy man with a long, black beard, holding a sword to Myanna's throat. His toothless smile held no warmth, as he watched their every move over her shoulder.

'Move, and I'll kill 'er,' he snarled.

Myanna flinched as the sword dug deeper into her skin, drawing blood.

'Don't you dare hurt my mother.' Amber stalked forward as she watched the trickle of blood flow down Myanna's neck and soak into the collar of her dress.

'Well ain't it all about the mothers today? First off, I get to meet the mother of Nikita's prize,' he squeezed Myanna tighter until she cried out, 'and I 'ear that lover boy's mam is none other than my queen's despicable sister. Somethin' I'm sure she'll be dead interested to 'ear.'

Connor moved closer and held his sword out to his side, 'You won't leave this forest alive. You know it and I know it, so why not do yourself a favour and let her go.'

The bearded man laughed, 'Ain't gonna happen.' He pulled Myanna along, pressing the sword deeper as he went. The look of terror on her face was too much for Amber.

'Wait!' she cried. 'Take me instead.'

The man stopped moving. 'I'm the prize that Nikita wants, so let my mother go and take me instead.'

'No Amber!' Redka grabbed her arm, but she jerked it free.

'Redka, please, let me do this.' She turned away from the bearded man to speak to Redka and Connor in a hushed voice. 'You, Connor, and Mags can work out how to get me out, but if I don't go, then this man will kill my mother. I've only just got her back.'

Connor ran his hands through his hair and paced back and forth, 'This is insane, Amber. If you go with him, Nikita will start extracting your powers and we might not get to you in time.'

'I know it's risky, but if I'm in the castle I can check on my dad. Cass and Tom will return soon with help, and you can all storm in and save us.'

She folded her arms across her chest to signify that she was not going to be swayed from her decision. The boys noted this and dropped their heads in defeat.

'Let her go, and I'll come quietly,' Amber shouted to the man.

CHAPTER 10

Tom had always wondered what it would feel like to be bewitched. As he stood in front of Rana, the Dragon Keeper, he believed he had found his answer.

She was a petite young woman, with a mass of red hair that framed her ivory face. A smattering of freckles ran across her nose, highlighting her bright-green eyes. She was mesmerising, and Tom struggled not to stare at her so intensely.

Cass approached the Keeper and bowed her head in greeting. 'Thank you for seeing us Rana. We come with news of Roth and the fortunes of Avaveil.'

Rana smiled warmly at them. She motioned for Cass and Tom to join her on the cushioned sofa that curved around the entire circumference of the creamy-coloured turret room.

'I have found it difficult to connect with Roth over the past few weeks. His spirit is weak, and I fear he is in incredible pain.' Rana's eyes filled with tears, and Tom had to fight the overwhelming impulse to hug her.

'We believe he is being subdued by a herbal potion that is inducing a dream state. This would explain why your mind link may not be working.'

Tom held up a hand, 'Sorry, can I just ask, what's a mind link?'

Rana studied Tom for a long while, and he began to wonder if she hadn't heard him, when suddenly he could hear her quite clearly in his mind.

I can mind link with anyone who is in the dragon realm, and with the dragons themselves.'

'That's so cool!' Tom cried, blushing as Cass and Rana burst out laughing.

As Rana tucked her legs underneath her on the sofa, Tom was reminded of all the nights he and Amber had hung out in her bedroom talking or listening to music. He hoped she was safe, and that his mission would be helpful for their cause.

'It is so nice to be able to surprise someone,' Rana was saying. Tom dragged himself back to the moment, and grinned at the Keeper.

'Even after everything I've seen, I still get giddy around people's gifts,' he admitted.

'I think it is lovely, Tom, and I hope we can keep surprising you during your stay in our realm.'

Cass steered the conversation back around to Roth and the cruel things Nikita was doing within the castle walls.

'She is draining the realm leaders of their powers and leaving them for dead. The only good news I can give you is that Roth is proving to be a difficult subject for Nikita's necromancer.'

'Roth will not give over his powers without a fight, of this I am most certain. You talked of the water sprite, Ninette. Is she recovering well?'

'When we left Avaveil she was still quite weak, but improving each day. Alia was hoping to arrange for her to be returned to the Great Sea as soon as possible. Being with her people would surely help her recovery.'

'Yes, I agree. I met Ninette's father about two hundred years ago. He was such a warm leader, and I know he would have instilled his strength upon his daughter. I do hope she makes a full recovery. You also mentioned Xavier.'

'Unfortunately, Xavier didn't survive,' Cass said. 'The orc leader perished soon after the extraction procedure.'

'That is such a shame; he was a powerful orc, and his death will have huge repercussions amongst the towns in the desert plains.'

A loud roar filled the air, and a heavy thump echoed through the turret as it shook. Tom leapt to his feet.

'Do not worry Tom, it is just Sali. She tends to land quite heavily on the roof although she is such a graceful flyer.' Rana stood and walked to the back of the circular room. There was a small archway cut into the stone and a short corridor beyond. 'Come,' she beckoned them to follow her.

Cass and Tom followed through the archway and along the short covered corridor. They ascended a set of stairs that led to an open air courtyard. The purple mountains rose high above them, and the tall pine trees coated the mountainside. The open area was about the size of playing field, with a sheer drop to the left.

'Don't go near the edge,' Cass whispered to Tom as she looked around at their surroundings.

Tom nodded emphatically. He kept his back to the mountain and walked across the courtyard to look back at the turret. Perched on the roof was a huge red dragon. Her leathery hide shone in the sunlight. Immense wings rose up from her back as she stretched and yawned. Tom swallowed hard at the sight of countless rows of sharp teeth.

'Now she's impressive,' he muttered under his breath.

The dragon swung its long neck in their direction and hopped off the roof to land heavily in the middle of the courtyard. She swivelled her head towards Tom, and he was convinced that she was smiling.

'Thank you,' she said, 'I'm inclined to agree with you.'

Tom jumped back, 'You can talk?'

Sali stalked forward on massive feet, her claws clipping on the flagstones of the courtyard as she moved.

'Of course I can talk. What were you expecting?'

Tom stammered with his words, as the dragon dropped her head so she was face-to-face with him. Her head was about three times the size of Tom's and he felt his knees begin to buckle as he eyed the rows of sharp teeth.

'I…I've never met a dragon before, so please accept my apologies if I've offended you.' His shoulder blades touched the rock behind him, and he sagged against the cold stone, finding some comfort in the sturdiness of the mountain.

Sali cocked her head to one side and winked at him, 'I do love a polite human. They taste so good.'

Rana appeared at Tom's side and placed a calming hand on his arm, 'Don't mind Sali. She likes to tease my guests.'

Tom realised he had been holding his breath, and let out a whooshing gasp as he tried to relax his shoulders. Sali chuckled and moved across the courtyard to where the stone dropped away. He concentrated all his efforts on getting his limbs to propel him the short walk to where Cass stood giggling at his predicament.

'It's not funny,' he complained as he finally reached her side.

'I know, I'm sorry.' She laced her fingers through his and squeezed his hand. He looked down at their entwined hands and grinned, his nervousness melting away.

'I've called the dragons to the Great Hall,' Sali told them, 'We will meet tonight and discuss your proposition to offer aid to the fae. You are welcome to join us there at nightfall.'

'Thank you, Sali. Until tonight.' Rana raised a hand to wave, as Sali rolled off the edge of the courtyard. Within seconds she soared up into the sky, her tremendous wings outstretched and beating a path towards the highest peak of the purple mountain.

TOM RECLINED on the grass with the waters of the lake lapping over his toes. He watched the indigo clouds drift slowly past, and listened to the gentle sound of the water. For the first time in a very long while, he was relaxed. Since his adventure with the Guardians of Phelan, it had been a difficult task to fall asleep at night. Instead, he lay awake, reliving the nightmare over and over. He had tried to explain how he felt to Amber, but she was duty-bound to return him and Connor to Hills Heath, whether they wanted to go back or not.

Sitting up to look out across the water, he caught sight of a family of dragons circling in the air on the far side of the lake. The biggest of the beasts lifted the tiny form of a baby dragon with his snout, and helped him rise above the top of a pine tree. His little wings flapped wildly as he tried to stay airborne. Tom's throat closed up as he took in the scene. This place filled him with such a strong sense of belonging that it overwhelmed him.

'Can I join you?' Cass appeared from the water's edge, her trousers rolled up to the knee and her feet submerged in the clear water.

Tom cleared his throat and patted the grass beside him, 'Of course you can.'

They sat in silence for a while watching the dragon family and listening to the sounds of the pine forest.

'I like you Tom,' Cass said in a hushed voice.

He twirled the long grass he was holding between his fingers and smiled, 'I feel the same.'

She leant across and kissed his cheek, but he stopped her before she could pull away.

'This is how we do it in the human realm.' He held her face between his hands and kissed her gently on the lips.

'I might have to visit this human realm,' she teased.

'This particular human never plans on leaving, so you won't need to make that trip.'

She snuggled against him, and he wrapped his arm around her shoulder. They sat that way for a long time; staring out over the water until the light began to fade, and the stars came out.

THE GREAT Hall was everything Tom had expected. It was carved out of a mountain; the entrance to it was the gaping mouth of a cave, with tall columns chiselled on either side. Carved into the stone and entwined around the columns were two dragons, who flanked the entrance and acted as defenders to all those who passed beneath the overhanging rock.

The cave was immense, and snaked into the heart of the mountain. Flaming torches led the way into the belly of the hall. Dragons of every size imaginable filled the area. Cass and Tom had travelled with Cass's family, and wound their way along the cave's edge so as not to be trampled by the gigantic feet of the dragons. Tom could see Rana in the distance, standing on a high, rising stone platform. Sali was with her, and they were joined by a dark-green dragon, who was even bigger than Sali.

'That's Yovan,' said Cass, noticing where Tom was looking, 'He is the next in command after Roth.'

Behind the stone platform was the dark shape of the mountain's heart. There were carvings covering the entire expanse of wall; dragons in flight over a burning city, dragons crossing an ocean, dragons soaring in the sky, and over burning forests.

'The carvings represent the different ages of the realm. Many leaders have tried to conquer the dragon realm, and every time they have been defeated,' said Cass, 'There was once a large settlement in this realm, whose people built a vast city and carved this great hall. Legend tells of an evil magician who turned the people against the dragons. There was a huge war, and the dragons were forced to vanquish the settlers and drive the magician back to the Lost Lands.'

'I'm surprised the dragons allowed your family to settle here after that,' Tom observed.

'Queen Alia and her father forged a great union with Roth and Yovan, and were able to rebuild the trust between our realms. My family was invited to stay, and keep the links open between Avaveil and the dragon realm. With Rana's help, these lands have stayed peaceful for centuries.'

'Out of interest, how old is Rana?'

'About six hundred years, give or take.'

Tom whistled, 'She doesn't look a day over twenty.'

Cass giggled, 'I bet you say that to all the great sorcerers.'

The huge basins that flanked the stone platform burst into flame, as Sali and Yovan exhaled their fire, omitting a deep rumble to silence the great hall.

Rana lifted her arms to the ceiling of the cave, and suddenly Tom could hear her in his head again.

My dearest family, our fae friends have brought us grave news about Roth. He is being held in the castle of Avaveil by Nikita, daughter of Javan. My mind link cannot reach him, and I fear he is in distress. It is the aim of the fae to reclaim the faerie throne, return Queen Alia to her rightful place, and bring honour to Javan's memory.

It is for us to decide on this night, if we will fly out on the morrow to fight with our friends and rescue our brother.'

There was a deep rumble as the dragons began to growl. The noise rose to a crescendo; each roar bouncing off the stone walls and amplifying.

'They are in agreement,' Cass shouted over the din to Tom.

'How do you know?'

'If they weren't, then they would just leave. The noise is a good sign. It means they are ready for a fight.'

THE FOLLOWING morning was bright and sunny, and Tom walked along the water's edge. The meeting in the Great Hall had lasted most of the night, as Rana and Yovan decided who should fight and who should guard the realm. Sali was returning to Avaveil with them and was receiving her final orders. Rana had called Cass and Tom to the turret at dawn to wish them luck on their journey. She bestowed a mind link upon them, so that they could connect with her at any time. Tom had been slightly apprehensive about having a six hundred-year-old sorcerer on speed dial to his brain, but Cass convinced him of the merits.

'Rana will sense if you are in danger and be able to send a dragon to your aid. Surely this is a wonderful relief as we head to war,' Cass had told him.

Tom hadn't thought about this great quest as a war until that moment. He tossed a stone across the water, and watched it leap frog across the glassy surface of the lake. He made a vow to himself right then. If he survived this war he was not returning to Hills Heath. He was going to live here in the dragon realm. He just had to find a way to tell Amber.

Sali dropped down on the grass behind him, causing him to drop his skimming stones and cry out.

She chuckled. 'Sorry to scare you.'

He held up one hand as he laid his other across his chest, feeling to check that his heart was still beating and hadn't exploded from fright.

'I don't think I'll ever get used to how a dragon can sneak up on you.'

Sali snorted and blew a blaze of fire out across the water.

'That's my warning sign. I can do that every time I approach if you like.'

Tom put his hands on his hips, and looked across at where the water bubbled as it boiled.

'Nope, it's fine. I'll just have to get used to you dropping in.'

She lowered her large head, so her chin was resting on the grass and dipped her wing towards him.

'Better hold on tight then, young Tom, we've got a long flight ahead.'

Tom's mouth hung open as he tried to find the appropriate words, 'You want me to sit on your back while you fly up there,' he pointed to the sky.

'How else are you planning to get to Avaveil as quickly as possible? If you walk, it will take another three days. If we fly, we can be there tonight.'

He took a deep breath and gingerly placed his right foot on Sali's wing, pulled himself up, and sat straddled on her neck.

'Hold on tight,' she said, as they launched into the air.

Tom clung to her neck and forced his eyes shut, muttering under his breath as the wind tore past his face. He heard his name being called in the distance, and dared to open one eye. Yovan soared through the air alongside Sali, his green scales twinkling in the bright sunlight. While Tom tried to focus on his gigantic form, he saw Cass was sitting on his back. She waved and turned her face into the wind, her hair flying out behind her. She whooped with glee, as Yovan dipped and twisted towards the white curtain and the gateway to Avaveil.

'Oh God, I'm going to die,' Tom muttered, as he shut his eyes.

CHAPTER II

Amber's limbs ached from being jostled along the dirt road by the bearded man. He was relentless in his goal to reach the castle and had pushed on without a break. Amber was feeling dizzy from exhaustion. The point of his sword pressed against the small of her back and stung with each step she took. She made a mental note to break his nose at the first opportunity she got.

As they rounded the bend in the road, the castle of Avaveil rose up ahead of them. Its turrets and walls gleamed in the midday sun. Amber was amazed at how serene the place looked, despite the evil that she knew resided within. A smaller road broke away from the main route into town and led up to the main gates. The space was crowded with minotaurs who quickly parted to line the edges of the track, as black beard marched his prize past them. Amber held her chin up and kept her eyes focused on the golden gates that loomed before her.

THE INTERIOR of the castle was gloomy in contrast to the bright day. Any light was extinguished with the loud crash of the doors slamming behind her. The bearded mercenary grabbed her arm and shoved her towards an open door. Stumbling briefly, she flashed him a look of disdain as she recovered her footing. She was herded into a large room with a broken window. A single throne, covered in colourful cushions, dominated the space. A long wooden table had been pushed against the far wall in an attempt to cover the gaping hole in the glass. The room was empty except for a pile of rags. As Amber watched, the rags moved and groaned. The bearded man marched across and swiftly kicked the mound of cloth. A sharp cry echoed around the stone room, and recognition flickered across Amber's face.

'Dad!'

The rags turned over, and Alan's bruised face lifted from the floor. She rushed to his side and flung her arms around him. With a weak grip, he clung to her and sobbed into her shoulder.

'What happened to you?'

'You must escape, Amber,' he said in a whisper, 'Leave me and save yourself, I beg you.'

The bearded man laughed as he stood over the two figures. 'Daddy don't look so good.' He swung his boot back and kicked Alan hard in the ribs.

Amber was on her feet in a second, her fist connected with the dirty man's nose, and she felt the bones break. Blood spurted down the man's face, and he stumbled backwards clutching his face with grubby hands.

Wasting no time, she pulled her powers forward until her hands were trembling. Great orbs of fire balanced in the palms of her hands and the bearded man's eyes shone with fear as she approached him.

Before she could burn the soul from this creature, her fire faded and she dropped to the floor clutching her head.

'Beautiful work,' said Nikita as she walked up to Amber's cowering form. Her hand was still outstretched as she held Amber in her magical vice.

Nikita glanced over to the mercenary, who nursed his broken nose as he cursed under his breath.

'How is it possible that *you* have brought my dear Amber here?'

The bearded man looked confused, 'She's the one you wanted, ain't she?'

'Oh, yes my dear fellow, don't get me wrong. Amber is indeed the most precious of trophies. I merely enquire as to how you survived. Aaron crawled through my gates earlier with tales of an ambush and a massacre. He saw *all* his men butchered and yet here you are.' She narrowed her eyes.

'We *was* ambushed. Them fae folk shot us with arrows. We scattered, but they was everywhere. Up every tree and behind every bush, 'undreds of em. The captain weren't there though, he'd gone to scout ahead of us.'

'How interesting.' Nikita released Amber from her magic and pressed her fingertips together as she circled around the bearded man. 'What else can you remember?'

The man gestured at Amber with a bloody hand, 'I over'eard this one talkin' with her faerie boyfriend about Alia.'

Nikita stopped walking and glowered at Amber, who lay panting on the floor.

The man continued, 'The boyfriend is Alia's boy, and they was the ones who killed everyone.'

In one fluid movement, Nikita grabbed the bearded man by the throat and lifted him into the air. His legs kicked out as he was suspended, and he clawed at Nikita's hands in a bid to free himself from her grasp.

'You lie!' she shouted at the man, squeezing his throat tighter.

'No, my queen, it's true,' the man gasped the words out, 'Alia is 'ere in Avaveil and she's got a son.'

The sound of his neck snapping filled the air. Nikita flung the body to one side and rounded on Amber. She lifted her palms and Amber rose from the floor to dangle in mid-air, frozen in the magical grip.

'Does that man speak the truth? Is my sister alive?'

Amber laughed as she hung in the air. She had tried to pull her power through, but whatever magic Nikita was using on her was thwarting her. The only form of attack left to her was knowledge.

'Yes, Alia's alive. She's here in Avaveil and can't wait to be reunited with her little sister.' Sarcasm dripped off every word as Amber watched Nikita's face grow even paler. 'She knows what you did,'

Amber went on, 'You arranged for her disappearance and then burnt her realm to the ground. But you didn't expect her to survive did you? Well, she did, and she's not alone.'

Nikita threw Amber across the room, where she landed heavily against the stone wall. With the wind knocked out of her, she gasped for breath, as Nikita tore across the room towards her. Thinking fast, she filled her mind with the red haze that Lavanya had taught her, and pressed her palms flat against the walls.

Before Nikita could reach for her, the stones of the castle began to shake. Dust particles rained down from the ceiling, as cracks appeared. The floor vibrated, and the remaining glass shattered, showering them with tiny shards.

Nikita wobbled and threw her hands out to steady herself, as the flagstones bucked and broke beneath her feet.

Amber could hear the cries of the guards outside the room as they hammered on the door to get in. Beyond the broken window, she could see the air turning orange. Flames began to lick across the floor and creep up the walls towards the ceiling. A deep rumble filled the air, and screams floated on the wind from the courtyard below.

'STOP!' Nikita had recovered herself, and now stood in the centre of the room holding Alan by the throat. Amber disconnected her energies and the castle grew silent once more. The flames extinguished, and the blue sky shone through the orange haze as it dissipated.

'Please don't hurt him.' She held her hands up in surrender. Her father's eyes bulged in their sockets as Nikita squeezed his throat, cutting off his oxygen supply.

The minotaur guards burst through the door and brandished their spears at Amber, circling her and obstructing her view of Nikita and her father.

'Dad!' she shouted over the throng of Nikita's guard.

They prodded her to rise from her position on the floor, and when she stood up both Nikita and Alan were gone.

THE GUARDS didn't take her to the dungeon as she had expected. Instead, Amber was led down a long corridor to the deepest part of the castle. The guards had shackled her arms and legs, and she was forced to shuffle. Her chains were heavy, and coated with a pungent syrupy substance that burnt when it touched her skin. The corridor ended at a large iron door. There were four guards on either side of the passageway, and Amber didn't think they were just here to watch over her.

The door screeched as it was opened from within, and a huge man with a bald head and black teeth filled the door frame.

''ello, little eye,' he said, 'welcome to my domain.' He ushered the guards to bring her inside.

There were no windows in this part of the castle, and the only light came from torches burning brightly along the outer wall. The room was long and thin, with shackles attached intermittently to the stone walls. A skeleton hung from the nearest set of chains, and Amber swallowed hard as they pushed her past.

A loud roar filled the room, and Amber flinched and threw her hands up to cover her ears. The guards held their spears out and shuffled nervously as they searched the darkness.

The bald man chuckled, 'Don't mind 'im. My other guest is a bit out o' sorts today. That little tremor you felt earlier broke his bonds, and we've 'ad to find other ways to restrain 'im.'

The guards pushed Amber ahead and she stared into the darkness, looking for any sign of the dragon. As they reached the far wall, she could see a single cell buried into the stone. The iron doorway stood open. To the right of the cell, the room opened up into a large cave with a low ceiling. Amber stopped behind the bald man as he gestured towards the cave.

'Incredible, ain't he?'

Her eyes had adjusted to the dim light, and she watched in shock as ten men hammered metal stakes into the ground. Each stake was attached to a huge chain which ran from one side of the cave to the other. Caught in the chains was the most beautiful creature Amber had ever seen. The dragon was pure white in colour with blood red eyes. Its head had been bound to the floor, sealing its mouth closed. It grunted and tried to lift its immense frame, but the chains were tight, biting into his hide.

'The mighty Roth,' the bald man strode over to the dragon and knelt down to whisper in his ear, 'looks like you get the day off, my friend, as Nikita's found another toy to play with.'

Roth lifted his gaze to meet Amber, and she felt a single tear spill down her cheek.

Laughing loudly, the bald man shoved Amber into the cell and slammed the door behind her.

'Don't get any ideas, little eye. Your magic won't work down 'ere and I'll be watching.' He tapped a huge dirty finger across his nose before swinging around to march out of the room with the guards in tow.

Amber slid down the rock wall and landed heavily on the ground, a sob escaping her.

'Now would be a great time to rescue me guys,' she mumbled, but there was no one around to hear her plea.

AARON STRETCHED his arm above his head, and cleaned the wound that he had instructed Connor to give him. The cut ran along his rib cage on the opposite side to where Amber had struck him with his dagger. It was becoming a frequent habit to have these people hurt him.

The door to his room opened, and Nikita breezed in, her long black dress swishing along the floor as she walked.

She shook her head as she examined the cut on his side, 'My poor Aaron. Those beasts are so cruel. If they weren't so petulant, I would recruit them for my mercenary army.' She laughed at her joke as she bathed a cloth in the bowl of water and dabbed at Aaron's wound.

He watched her warily, 'My queen, you do not need to tend to my injury.'

She waved a hand to dismiss his comment, 'My bravest of captains should be cared for.' She carried on cleaning his wound.

Eventually she threw the cloth on the table, and Aaron pulled his tunic down with a short nod of his head, 'Thank you.'

'You are most welcome,' she said, moving towards the small window seat that provided a comfortable spot to look out over the forest. 'Tell me Aaron, how is it that you were able to escape such a bloody battle with merely a scratch?'

'My queen?'

'There was another survivor,' she paused and seated herself on the window seat, 'A horrid little man with a scruffy black beard. He managed to escape the gruesome fight and make it back to the castle.' She folded her hands in her lap and appraised him.

'I am overjoyed, my queen. Tell me where I can find him, and I will congratulate him on his escape.'

'He died soon after his arrival.' She waved her hand absent-mindedly before going on,

'Before he perished I was able to speak with him about an interesting development. You see, it appears my beloved sister has returned to the realm.'

'Impossible! It has been many years since her disappearance, and you told us she was dead.'

She stood up and walked over to where he sat perched on the table, her eyes never leaving his.

'I know what I told you, but I lied. I feared she was dead, but didn't have the proof. It was in the realm's best interest that a queen sat on the throne. You understand don't you Aaron?'

'Yes, my queen.'

'Good, I am glad to hear it because a queen needs her loyal captains to stand by her side in times of great crisis.' She ran her fingers through his hair. 'Of course, if I were to discover that any of my captains were not loyal, then I would have no choice but to remove them from my service, don't you agree Aaron?'

He nodded in agreement, but Nikita caught a handful of his hair and pulled his head back sharply. She leaned over him and through clenched teeth spoke, 'There is a boy, a son of Alia that must die. They must not be allowed to enter this castle. If Alia makes it through those gates, then we will all die.'

She released her hold on his hair, and he collapsed across the table.

'I ask that you pick your best men and send them out into the forest to kill these miscreants.'

He rubbed the back of his head as he rose from the table, 'I will see to it personally, my queen, and I assure you that none shall survive.'

'Ah, my sweet Aaron, you will send out your men, but you will not be joining them. I have need of your skills here. Our survivor was able to bring a gift back for his queen before meeting an untimely death, and as you are now my only necromancer I will need you to perform an extraction.'

'An extraction? Just who did this barbarian manage to capture?'

Nikita's smile was cruel as she pulled open the door to his room, 'This barbarian was able to bring me exactly what I asked for, unlike his captain.'

Aaron stuttered to find the words to answer.

'Do not fret Aaron, I need your necromancer skills to extract Amber's powers. You are only alive because I still need you.'

She swung open the door so he could see the guards posted at his door, 'Just in case you had any ideas about warning your little faerie friends.'

Aaron slumped against the table, his shoulders hunched over in defeat. He was on borrowed time now, and there was nothing more he could do to help Alia.

AMBER WATCHED the men collect their tools and leave the room. Their bodies were drenched in sweat from the exertion of hammering in the nails that would bind Roth to the castle floor. They muttered amongst themselves as they left, and Amber caught the odd word as they filed past her cell. 'Alia' and 'son' were the two that stood out the most.

She rested her back against the cool stone wall and hugged her knees to her chest. If Nikita knew that Alia and Redka were in Avaveil, then the war was about to begin.

'Are you hurt, little eye?' The voice was so soft that Amber almost missed it.

She lifted her head, half expecting someone to be stood just outside the cell door, but the space was empty. She couldn't see anyone in the room. She moved position so she could kneel and peer through the bars into the cave.

'Roth?'

'Yes it is I. Are you hurt?'

Amber's heart filled with warmth as she looked at the huge beast, who despite his suffering, was concerned for her welfare.

'No, I'm not hurt. Nikita needs me in good working order so she can extract my powers. Are you in much pain?'

'Pain is a figment of the imagination, and I have no need to imagine it at this time. I would very much like to lift my head though.'

'Wouldn't you be able to blast them all with fire if your head were free?'

'Indeed, that is the very reason I wish to lift my head.'

Amber laughed, 'For the record, I wish you could lift your head too.'

A soft rumble vibrated through the floor as Roth chuckled. 'I almost managed it earlier. The castle shook and my bindings broke, but thanks to the herbal mixture they spoon fed me I wasn't fast enough to respond. They had me chained before the castle stopped its shaking.'

'That was my fault I'm afraid. One of the oracle powers I have is glamour, and I connected with the stone to try and break the walls. Nikita threatened my father, so I had to stop.'

'Is there no way for you to access your powers now?'

'I tried, but they've coated my chains with some syrup, and if I try to access my energy, the stuff burns into my skin and releases a strong smell that chokes me.'

'They have bound your shackles with black magic. It is the same for me.'

They were silent for a time as they both pondered their respective predicaments.

'Queen Alia and her group of warriors are not far away and they plan to rescue me. I know that my friend Tom has travelled to your realm in the hope that the dragons will come to assist.' She hoped that this would offer Roth some small comfort.

'If my brothers and sisters enter Avaveil then I will know it. We share a link through our minds with the Keeper of our realm. I have had no such connection, so I fear that your Tom has been unsuccessful.'

'Give them time, Roth. We've both got to focus on staying positive.'

The door at the far end of the room opened, and a stream of guards poured through. At the centre, surrounded by swords, was Aaron. His hands were bound and his face was covered in blood. They reached the cell, and one of the guards unlocked her door.

'What happened to you?' Amber asked, as she was dragged to her feet to stand beside him.

'Let's just say Nikita doesn't like the company I have been keeping lately.'

'She did this to you?'

'No, she wouldn't get her hands dirty. This is the work of a very large, bald gentleman who specialises in torture.'

'Are you a prisoner too, then?'

Aaron looked at her through bloodshot eyes, encircled by dark smudges. There was a deep gash above his ear and his white hair was matted with blood. Amber looked at his hands that were covered in bruises and lacerations. His knuckles looked like he had been dragged through glass.

'I am a prisoner of sorts. Nikita has sent me to extract your powers.'

Amber took a step backwards, but bumped into a guard who held her shoulders tightly. She shook her head as her eyes darted around the room. 'No, you can't do this.'

'I have to Amber. Otherwise, she will kill your father.'

Amber felt her legs give way, and she pitched forward. The guard grabbed her before she hit the ground, and swung her over his shoulder. They marched off towards the exit.

Amber bounced along staring at the floor and the guard's legs, trying to come up with a plan of escape, but her mind emptied of everything but the sensation of being jostled.

Before they left the room, she lifted her head to see Roth watching her. He strained his head against his binding, blood pouring over his snout as the chain cut him.

She gave him a sad smile before he disappeared from view.

CHAPTER 12

Redka's eyes drooped as he rested his head on the table in the lord's living room. His mother was meeting with Mags to coordinate the rescue that was set for that night, and he had been told to stay behind in the village.

'I need to help,' he had explained to his mother, but she was adamant that he and Amber stay apart, telling him that Connor and Mags were capable of bringing her back safely. It was too much for him. He had shouted at Alia for a long time, trying everything in his power to change her mind, but to no avail.

His head felt heavy as his eyes fluttered closed, and deep sleep crept over him.

'DO NOT *be afraid, young Prince, you are safe.'*

Redka opened his eyes and studied his surroundings. The brightness of the clouds caused him to squint until he could adjust to the sudden light.

'Where am I?'

'I have brought you to the oracle realm because I need your help.'

He sat upright and looked at the mystical woman who stood in front of him. She was beautiful. Her long silver hair hung over her shoulders and was almost as long as the white robes she wore. A silver charm hung around her neck.

'Lavanya?'

She nodded. 'My link with Amber has been broken and I am unable to reach her. Her future is clouded, and when I search for her I find only fire.'

'What does that mean? Is she still alive?'

She lay a small hand on his arm to offer some comfort, 'She is still alive, but she is hidden from view by very dark magic. We must act quickly before she is lost to the darkness.'

'The darkness? What does that mean?'

'The prophecy is clear. The last oracle will unite the realms, but only if she can control her emotions and not lose herself in the dark. If she uses her powers to defeat Nikita, there is every possibility that she will lose her soul along with it, and an alternative prophecy will come to pass; one in which will see your realm, and every other realm, burn.'

'Amber wouldn't do that,' he snapped.

'If she loses control then she will be unaware of what she is doing, and inadvertently kill us all. Her strength lies in your bond. You can act as her anchor to the light. Keep her steady and able to use her strength to win this war. Isha has bestowed a great power upon her, but she is too volatile to control it.'

She knelt down in front of Redka and held his hands in her own, 'Amber is a sixteen-year-old girl. She loves with boundless passion and she hurts with equal intensity. This side of her needs to be guided. Her oracle powers are incredible, but she has not the skill, nor experience to handle them. Her oracle gift was meant to be nurtured by a loving family, to grow over time and develop. But Amber has had this thrust upon her in the throes of madness, and I fear that it will overwhelm her, and she will be lost to us all.'

'What can I do?' Redka asked his voice nothing more than a whisper.

'Go to the castle, rescue her, and bring her back safely where we can guide her next steps.'

'My mother won't allow it, she has seen a vision. She thinks Amber will harm me.'

'My Prince, it is not Amber who will cause you harm. The warrior your mother has sensed in her dreams is another. You must get to Amber, and together you will be able to prevail. Your strength lies in this union.'

THE SOUND of the door opening stirred Redka from his dreams. Alia watched him with affection and bent over to kiss the top of his head.

'I'm sorry I disturbed you. These past few weeks have been tiring on all of us.'

'I have to go.' He jumped up from the table, reached for his sword, and stopped and knelt before Alia, 'Mother, my queen, I ask for your forgiveness, but I am going with the others to rescue Amber.'

Alia began to protest, but Redka cut her off, 'Lavanya has visited me, and it is imperative that I reach Amber first. She will not harm me.'

'I've seen it Redka,' she reached for his arms and clung to him, 'The warrior will harm the prince. I see it over and over.'

'That warrior you speak of is not Amber. She needs me mother, and I must go.'

'If Amber is not the warrior, then who could it...oh.'

'I promise to be careful and return to you.' He kissed his mother lightly on the cheek and then walked out of the living room and down the wooden stairs, his feet moving quickly as he rushed to catch up with Connor and Mags.

THE LEATHER straps cut into Amber's wrists and ankles. The minotaurs had bound her tightly, and movement was impossible. The disgusting syrup that held her magical abilities in check coated the table top and the restraints.

Aaron stood over her, and he looked nervously at the guards who circled the table watching his every move. There was no way to do this without causing Amber pain.

He dropped his dagger, and when he stooped down to retrieve it, he whispered quickly into Amber's ear.

'This will cause great pain, I am sorry. I don't know what power to take and still leave you with your strength.'

Amber thought quickly, and as Aaron stood against the table she tried to buck against her restraints, two of the guards stepped forward and slammed her back against the table, rattling her bones in the process. She clenched her teeth and shouted, 'Don't you *dare* take my healing powers, I can't live without them.' She looked pointedly at Aaron, who gave the smallest nod of his head as he understood her message.

Taking her healing energy would mean that her body would heal at the same rate as a normal human and she would suffer pain; but once fully recovered she would still be strong and her elemental magic would be intact. It was a smart move, and Aaron was impressed with the way she controlled herself.

'Get a move on.' One of the guards prodded Aaron in the shoulder with the point of his spear causing Aaron to flinch.

'If I am to perform the extraction without killing Nikita's prize possession, then I advise you to refrain from sticking your blade in my flesh.'

The guard grunted and lowered his spear but remained at his post.

Aaron took a deep breath and began.

Amber's screams filled the corridors and carried down to Roth in the lower cave, who closed his eyes and wept.

THE GUARDS dumped Amber in her cell several hours later, dropping her to the floor without any care for the pain it caused her. The same pain that shot through her limbs like an electrical current. At the time, it had seemed the best option to prompt Aaron to take her healing energy. She had Myanna on hand to teach her about herbs after all. But what she hadn't realised was that along with her healing gift and knowledge, the extraction would also take away her ability to self-heal as quickly.

She wanted to sit up, and to reassure Roth that she was going to be okay, but her body wouldn't respond. Her arms throbbed where

Aaron had fed the needles into her veins. She could still feel the sensation of her powers being sucked out. Her blood boiled and burnt her insides as it swirled through her system. Eventually, the dark magic passed through her heart and was pumped back out to Aaron's waiting vial, ready for transportation to Nikita.

Her stomach lurched, and she vomited on the cell floor.

'Little eye?'

She wiped her mouth with the back of her hand and grabbed the bars of the cell. She used them to drag herself upright. The cold metal offered small comfort against her raging fever.

'I'm okay Roth. I'm alive.'

'I was so worried when I heard your screams. If I get free, I shall eat that white haired necromancer whole.'

Amber smiled, she didn't have the energy to laugh, 'Aaron is one of the good guys; he's just been placed in a bit of a predicament.'

'A good guy? That half-breed and the female necromancer used their dark magic to try and extract my powers. He didn't seem like he was one of the good guys then.'

'I think we've managed to change his mind. A few days ago he would probably have sold my soul to the devil, but today he tried everything he could not to kill me. Although it may end up getting him killed instead.'

'Well, if you can place your trust in him, then so can I.'

They stayed silent for a long while. Amber could hear the faint dripping of water as it slid off the cave wall and hit the flagstones below.

'Can you hear that?'

Roth grunted. 'Yes, the dripping has been driving me insane since I arrived in this place.'

'No, not the dripping. It sounds like marching feet.'

They listened intently until Amber was sure that the thud, thud, thud was the sound of an army on the move.

'If Nikita has sent out her army, then that means my friends must be close.'

Roth released a low grumble that vibrated through the bars of Amber's cell. She moved her head away from the metal and stared into the darkness, trying to see Roth's outline. His eyes glowed in the gloom.

'What is it Roth?'

'I hear them,' he said. 'I hear Sali and Yovan.'

'You can hear your family? Doesn't that mean...'

'Yes, they are here in Avaveil and they are coming.'

Amber did laugh this time. 'Good old Tom, I knew he wouldn't let me down.'

CONNOR POSITIONED himself on the highest branch he could find. The others did the same. To anyone passing through the forest, it would appear to be deserted. Mags signalled for the female warriors to ready their wings. They were in position, and all they had to do now was to wait. Nightfall was only an hour away, and once the sun set they would strike at the heart of the castle.

Redka nestled on the tree branch alongside Connor. 'Do you think she's okay?'

'Yeah, she's tough. Look at what she's come through already. A couple of hours in a dank cell won't break her.'

'Nikita might. From what the lord of the village has told us, she doesn't hold back with her evil magic. What if Amber doesn't have the strength to sustain this until nightfall?'

'What can we do Redka? We can't stroll up to the gate and demand that they give her back.' He pondered this for just a moment before shaking his head. 'No, it wouldn't work.'

'I could do it,' Redka offered.

'Are you crazy? Nikita would kill you before you put one toe over her doorstep.'

'She doesn't know who I am. I could tell her I have information about the band of faeries who ambushed her men, she will have to...'

He was cut off by the sound of the great golden gates opening.

'Sssh,' Connor hissed, dipping his body low against the branch. He gestured to Mags, who signalled for the warriors to ready themselves for attack.

As they watched the castle, a row of minotaur guards filed through the gates. They were four deep, and all heavily armed with spears and swords. They marched in unison down the dirt track and onto the road, heading towards the woodland village. Redka counted at least one hundred minotaurs.

Connor motioned to Heidi, one of the closest fae to his position. She spread her wings and manoeuvred her way through the overhanging branches to join him.

'I need you to go to the village, and warn Alia that an army is heading their way. It may be safer for her to join us here than to take on a hundred hairy beasts.'

She smiled and shot off into the sky, hurtling over the tree tops towards the lord's village.

'If the army has left, does that mean the castle is vulnerable?'

Connor shook his head and pointed to the curtain wall surrounding the courtyard. A swell of minotaurs still stood guard around the perimeter of the bailey.

'Nikita isn't that stupid. She's sent out a small section of her army in the hope that they will be enough to kill us. She wasn't banking on the fae standing behind Alia though.'

The two boys looked out across the treetops. As far as they could see, every tree was filled with faeries. Male warriors clutched their swords, and the female warriors hovered in the air with their arrows at the ready. Many of the fae folk had flocked to Alia's cause. They were ready to fight for the greater good, and vanquish Nikita and her murderous followers. They wanted to reclaim the realm for the fae folk and honour their dead. Hundreds had joined them following Mags' mission to spread the word. Even the fae from the furthest points of Avaveil had heard the whispers and come to fight.

The army rumbled off into the distance as the sky grew darker. Mags dropped soundlessly to the floor and signalled for the male warriors to move out. The female fighters were to attack from the sky and prevent anyone from escaping. A small minority were tasked with swooping in and taking out any injured.

'Let's go.' Connor rushed ahead with Redka close behind, with the rest of the fae bringing up the rear. They melted into the surroundings, hugging their bodies close to the grasses of the dried up moat. They circled around the perimeter of the castle and acted as one huge pincer.

On Mags' command they advanced, spilling through open windows, hacking down the guards at the main gate, and swarming through to the courtyard. They attacked with an eerie silence, and the minotaurs didn't hear them coming until it was too late.

Once inside the bailey, Connor and Redka hurried for the dungeon, leaving Mags to contend with the army of minotaurs that now poured from every crevice in the castle.

They ran as quickly as they could, clashing swords with a few guards who were unfortunate enough to cross their path.

The dungeon was in darkness as they stepped inside. Redka snatched up a torch and searched every cell looking for Amber.

'Connor?' a hoarse voice called out into the room.

Redka hurried the torch towards the sound. He expected to find Amber, but instead he found Aaron, shackled and beaten.

'What the hell happened?' Connor fished around the fallen minotaur guard for the keys, and quickly opened the cell door.

'Nikita discovered I had been helping Alia, and had me tortured.'

'Where's Amber?'

'She is on the other side of the castle, deep in the lower cells.' He grabbed Connor's arm. 'She's not good and it's all my fault.'

'What do you mean she's not good? What did you do Aaron?'

'It was Nikita; she made me start the extraction. If I didn't do as she said, then Amber's father would have died. We worked something out, Amber and I, but I know it cost her dearly.'

Through gritted teeth Connor pulled Aaron up to his feet. 'Take us to her.'

IT WAS slow going, as Aaron struggled with a leg injury. They wound their way through long corridors, and up and down flights of stairs, until coming to a dank corridor. At the end stood a large iron door, and in front of the door stood an even bigger bald man with a set of black teeth.

ALIA AND Myanna ran through the woods, following Heidi, as she made her way back to the castle and the faerie army. The lord of the village and the remaining village folk were huddled together in a tight group, trying to keep up with their queen.

'Majesty,' the rotund little lord panted as he caught up to Alia. 'Majesty, we are having trouble keeping this pace. Surely there is another option.'

Alia glanced around at the children and older faeries who had been left behind in the village. Her heart filled with an overwhelming urge to protect them.

'Come, follow me.' She ushered them deeper into the woods and found a cluster of oak trees. Their huge trunks formed a clear circle. Alia grouped the villagers together within the circle and gently moved the lord in after them.

'I can protect this circle of trees, and cast a shielding spell that will keep you safe, even if Nikita's army were to pass right by. They will not know you are there.'

The lord grabbed Alia's hand and kissed it, 'Thank you, my queen. May your powers be returned, and the throne be yours once more.'

Alia concentrated her energy on the group of oaks, and a shimmering curtain of light coated their trunks and leaves. As Myanna watched, the trees vanished from sight leaving nothing but open grassland.

'Where did they go?' she asked.

'Do not worry Myanna, they are still there but you can't see them. No one can.'

They began moving again, Heidi leading the way through the undergrowth.

'If you had left me behind, then you and Heidi could have flown to the castle,' Myanna grumbled.

'I'm not leaving my most talented healer behind. Or my most precious friend.' Alia laced her fingers through Myanna's and squeezed. 'We stick together.'

Myanna chuckled. 'Yes, my queen.'

THE CREAMY stones of the castle shone in the moonlight as they approached.

'Majesty, we must stay in the treeline.'

Alia stopped and gazed out at the castle, as Heidi motioned for them to climb the nearest tree.

'I haven't seen this place in ten years. Nikita has destroyed it.' Tears streamed down Alia's face as she took in the destruction that had once been her home.

'Majesty, please, I need you out of sight. Climb up and we can wait for Prince Redka to emerge.'

Myanna tugged on her arm, and they both began to climb, lifting themselves up the branches until they were safely hidden amongst the dense leaves.

'I wish you had seen this place when I ruled,' she whispered to Myanna. 'It was so beautiful. The stones gleamed in the sunlight, and the clear waters of the moat were a safe playground for the children. Market stalls would line the roadside, and brightly coloured wagons rolled through on their way to other realms and far off adventures.'

Myanna hugged Alia close to her side and let her weep.

'When you reclaim your throne, I will help you rebuild that world. I promise.'

Alia smiled, her watery eyes shining in the light of the moon. 'What of your family, your husband and Amber? They are your priority, Myanna.'

'I will deal with that later. For now, we have to get your castle back.' They sat in silence, listening to the sounds of fighting beyond the castle walls.

'What did the lord mean when he said, "may your powers be returned"?'

Alia pointed to the golden gates at the front of the castle. 'Do you see those gates? My father cast a spell centuries ago that made it possible for any fae king or queen to leave their magic essence within the carvings. If ever they lost the castle to an enemy, then a piece of our magic would reside in the very structure, growing in strength until we were able to return.'

Myanna gazed at the huge gates. 'If you were to touch those...'

Alia's eyes grew bright as she answered her friend. 'My full powers would be returned.'

They looked down at the gates from their secluded spot and watched the battle rage on. The fae warriors were equally matched by the guards, who were fighting hard to try and keep the fae from entering the castle. The gates stood open, as more minotaurs surged forward. Arrows flew in all directions, and the clash of metal on metal filled the night air.

'We have to find a way to get you down there,' Myanna said.

CHAPTER 13

I will deal with this.' Aaron stepped forward to face the giant man who barred their way. Redka handed him a sword and hung back, allowing the older warrior to approach his adversary.

Swinging the sword left and right Aaron sliced through the air in front of him. The bald man watched his opponent with interest.

'So you think you can 'urt me?' He spat on the floor and grinned, showing off his black smile. 'I'd like to see you try, faerie scum.'

Aaron continued whirling the sword back and forth, and inching closer to the man.

'There lies your first mistake,' Aaron said.

He stopped moving, and held the sword still between the palms of his hands, the blade aimed at the bald man's heart. 'You see I am only a half-faerie scum. The other half is necromancer.'

There was a blinding flash, and the blade spun forward at a terrific pace to land solidly in the bald man's chest. He careened through the iron door, flying through the air, and covering the long distance of the dark room beyond. There was a sickening crunch, as his immense bulk was impaled against the furthest stone wall.

A scream filled the air.

'Amber!' all three shouted in unison.

Redka sprinted through the doorway and headed for the sound of the scream. The room was long and dim, only lit by the flickering torches on the walls.

He ran frantically towards the dimly lit cell that was carved into the stone. A low growl echoed around the chamber, and he realised he was unarmed. Looking behind him he saw Connor closing in. He shouted for a weapon, and as they ran, Connor unhooked his dagger and threw it.

Everything seemed to happen in slow motion. Redka lost his footing on the uneven flagstones, and as he twisted his body to cushion his fall, the dagger flew straight and true and into his chest. He dropped to the floor like a boulder.

Connor cried out in warning, but it was too late. The dagger was buried deep in his heart. Aaron stumbled to a halt beside him, dropping to his knees, but shaking his head when he could feel no pulse.

'NO!' Amber was locked in the cell just a couple of metres from Redka's body, and she screamed hysterically as she watched him fall.

There was a loud rumbling to the right of the cells, and Connor noticed Roth for the first time. He was straining against his bonds, and blood poured down his leathery skin.

Connor was in a daze, everything felt a million miles away. He could hear Amber screaming, and Roth straining against his restraints. Aaron was shouting something to him, but he couldn't move. His limbs were too heavy and his head too full of noise.

The warrior will hurt the prince.

He clutched his head, as Alia's message rolled over and over in his brain. They had kept Amber and Redka apart for all those weeks when she wasn't the danger. He was.

Aaron's face filled his vision, as the faerie warrior grasped him by the shoulders and shouted at him.

'Connor! We have to move, get Amber out of the cell, and smash Roth's chains. We have to move now!'

Connor moved like he was on autopilot. He snatched the keys from the bald man's belt, as he hung lifelessly from the wall beside Amber's cell. He unlocked the door and flung it open. Amber pushed past him and threw herself at Redka, screaming all the time. Connor grabbed a heavy axe off the floor and swung the blade at the giant chains. One by one, they shattered, until Roth lifted his mammoth body off the floor. He opened his mouth and roared.

'DID YOU hear that?' Myanna clutched Alia's arm as the night air filled with an incredible sound.

'It's Roth. They have freed him.'

They squinted to see through the blackness of the night, but the moon was hidden behind the heavy cloud. The sounds of battle clung to them, as the chill in the air seeped into their bones.

'If Roth is free, then the battle will soon be over. He will tear them apart.'

As if on cue, the wall at the back of the castle crumbled and fell with a horrendous crash. Clouds of dust and rubble rose high into the sky. A column of fire lit up the grounds, and Alia could see Roth emerge from the crater. His immense white frame was covered with scars and blood poured down his snout. He unfurled his mighty wings and roared.

The minotaur army began to retreat, dropping their weapons and running to the golden gates in a bid to escape the onslaught of the dragon.

To the west of their position, a second roar carried on the winds, and then a third.

The army rushed in every direction as the dragons descended from the skies.

Alia turned to Heidi and pointed towards the castle. 'Can you get us to the gates?'

'Majesty, my orders were to keep you here.'

'Heidi, I need to reach the castle and unlock my full powers. I need you to get me there.'

The faerie looked out over the battlefield. Four huge dragons soared over the castle burning everything in their path, and fae warriors fought the minotaurs on the ground as they tried to escape. The female fighters guarded the sky alongside the dragons, pulling the injured from the heart of the castle and flying them to safety, while picking off any of Nikita's army that slipped past the defences.

The gates were at the very centre of the battle, but when Heidi looked at Alia, her eyes showed only strength and courage.

'I will try my best, Majesty.'

Alia smiled. 'Thank you, Heidi. I will carry Myanna with us, and I am counting on your skill with a bow to keep us out of danger.'

Alia spread her wings, the iridescent colours twinkling in the bright fires that burnt beyond the treeline.

'Ready?'

Myanna nodded as she clung to her friend. 'Ready as I'll ever be.'

They lifted off and spiralled towards the gate.

AARON CARRIED Redka's body over the rubble, as they followed Roth through the freshly made hole in the castle wall. Amber scrambled after him, her face covered in grime and tears. She cursed herself for giving up her healing powers so lightly. As Roth had punched his way through the solid wall, Aaron had found a faint pulse in Redka's neck. They had to get him to the forest and find Myanna.

Connor ran blindly on behind them, disoriented from the clouds of dust and the roar of battle. Amber had ignored him as they fled the dungeon, and he couldn't blame her. He may have just killed the Prince of Avaveil and her one true love.

The scene that unfolded as the group scaled the fallen masonry was hard to take in. Dragons and faeries filled the skies like guardians called to protect the weak. Their fire and arrows found enemy targets at every turn.

AARON PRESSED forward heading for the main gate. As they ran through the open courtyard, they were confronted by two large minotaurs. Both were panting hard from the exertion of fighting long and hard. Aaron was unable to protect them, and Amber had no weapon. Connor stepped ahead and brandished his sword. Before he could swing his blade, a huge roar sounded just above them, and a bright red dragon swooped down and snatched the guards from the ground in its large claws. Amber looked up in time to see Tom sitting astride the back of the giant beast.

'Let's go!' Aaron shouted, moving on.

The golden gates loomed ahead of them as they darted through the large entrance hall. Nikita's throne room was to the left, and as they rushed past, Amber glanced sideward and skidded to a halt. Aaron stumbled ahead, but stopped when Connor called out to him. The three of them stood in the doorway.

Nikita was wearing her finest dress. The long, black skirt cascaded from her tiny waist and tumbled onto the floor. The bodice of the dress fit snuggly against her body and the capped sleeves rose up to meet a high collar. Her long white hair flowed down her back and was framed by her obsidian crown. Under any other circumstances, Amber would have said she was stunning, but hanging limply from her outstretched hand was Alan Noble.

'Let him go Nikita, you've lost. The castle is under the control of the fae.'

'Oh no, my dear, I don't lose. I never lose.'

'You've lost this one. If you spare my father, then I'm sure Queen Alia will be lenient with your punishment.'

Nikita laughed and shook Alan. Amber started forward, but Connor grabbed her arm.

'My dear sister is no match for me. She hides in a dirty village with her filthy faeries and lets children fight her battles. Alia will be sorely disappointed when none of her loyal subjects return.'

Aaron slowly slid Redka's body off his shoulders, and laid him gently on the ground just beyond the doorframe. As he looked up towards the golden gates, he saw a flurry of arrows strike the two guards who remained at their post. Through the fog of the dragons' fire, he saw three figures approaching. Myanna rushed through the gates towards Redka, pulling her healing bag over her head as she ran. Aaron gestured for her to remain hidden from sight, and she nodded her understanding before slipping to the floor and pulling Redka out of the way.

Alia stood in front of the gates. Her incredible wings stretched to touch either side of the frame. Aaron could see a young faerie warrior in the background, letting off arrows as she protected her queen. Alia placed her hands on the gates, and a golden flash flooded the hallway. Aaron flung his arms up to protect his eyes. In the throne room, Nikita screamed.

'No!' She threw Alan to the side, and hurled herself towards the doorway, firing a bolt of magical energy at Connor as she ran. He flew backwards, hitting the wall with a sickening thud. Amber dropped to the ground and covered her head, but Nikita pushed past her and out into the entrance hall.

Aaron stood with his back to the wall, midway between where Alia stood facing Nikita.

A golden aura surrounded the queen as she walked forward under the archway of the golden gates and inside the castle.

Myanna kept her head down low and continued to work on Redka, applying salves and wrapping his wounds with herbs.

Nikita's eyes turned black as she stared at her sister.

'You have returned.'

'Yes, Nikita, I have returned and it is time for me to take back my throne.'

'The throne no longer recognises you as its queen, dear sister.'

Alia extended her hands and raised two golden orbs. 'I believe the throne disagrees with you.'

Pressing her fingertips together, Nikita rolled a green orb between her palms. 'If you want to play, then I am more than happy to trade blows. We used to have such fun when we were children.' Her cruel smile danced across her face.

'You never played fair, if I remember correctly,' Alia said, holding her magic steady.

Nikita laughed. 'No, I didn't did I?' She launched the green orb, but not at Alia. It flew through the air towards Myanna and Redka.

Amber screamed out in warning but the orb was right on target.

Aaron launched himself from the wall and threw his body in its path, blocking the magic. It exploded over him, as he dropped to the floor writhing in pain.

Alia didn't falter; she threw the golden orbs at her sister. They connected directly and engulfed her in a white flame. Nikita's screams were drowned out by the roar of the fire as it consumed her body. When the orbs blinked out, there was nothing but a pile of ash left on the floor.

AARON CRIED out as the dark magic seeped into his body. Amber rushed to his side as Myanna tried to direct her on how to help him.

'I don't have my healing powers; they were extracted.' They stared at each other over his squirming body and a silent understanding passed between them. Amber scooped his head off the floor and cradled him in her lap. She held his hand as he fought against the magic that was eating away at him.

'What's happening to him?'

Alia lowered herself to the floor between Redka and Aaron, checking on her son before turning to answer Amber.

'He is dying. The dark magic that my sister works with is killing him.'

'Can't you do something? Can't you take out the evil and put in that golden stuff?'

'I wish I could Amber, but it doesn't work that way.'

Aaron bucked and twisted on the floor and clenched his teeth.

'Amber.' His voice was hoarse, and his face was covered in a sheen of sweat. 'Remember that I had some good in me, remember that.'

'Of course I will remember that, you saved my life Aaron. You saved all of us. We will always remember you.'

His eyes fluttered, and he tightened his grip on her hand. With a final jolt, his body jerked, and he slumped back on the ground, silent.

Amber's shoulders rocked as she let the tears fall.

FROM THE opposite corner, Connor groaned and shifted his position. He held his head to try and stop the pounding in his brain. Myanna moved over to check on him, and left Alia to watch over her son.

'Is Redka okay?' Amber asked as she gently lowered Aaron's head to the floor.

'Yes, he will be fine. He is home now, and our royal magic will heal him quickly. Do not fear.'

'I couldn't help him, and I was so afraid I'd lose him again.'

Alia pulled Amber close. 'I owe you an apology. I kept the two of you apart because I truly believed you would be a danger to him. Your oracle powers were so unstable, and my vision was so clear, but...'

'Wrong warrior.'

'Indeed,' Alia agreed. 'Wrong warrior.'

A SHUFFLING sound drew their attention, and both Amber and Alia lifted their heads to see Alan Noble standing at the entrance to the throne room. He was silhouetted against the raging fires that plundered the courtyard outside, the orange glow giving him a vibrant aura. He only had eyes for one person.

'Hello, Myanna,' he spoke softly.

Myanna froze as she fixed a bandage to Connor's head, her hands trembled.

'It's okay, you can turn around,' Connor whispered to her.

She stood, and slowly spun around to face her husband. The man she hadn't seen in ten years. The one she was willing to forget in order to stay in Avaveil with Alia.

His face was bruised and bloody, and his hair was dishevelled. He had lost so much weight that his clothes hung off him, but Myanna couldn't tear her gaze away from his eyes. The same warm eyes that she had fallen in love with all those years ago. She ran to him, and flung her arms around his neck as she kissed him.

Amber smiled.

CHAPTER 14

The sounds of battle diminished as the minotaur army threw down their swords. With the dragons and fae guarding the sky, they could not win. The whisperings that Nikita was dead filled every corner, and so the surrender was swift.

Mags herded the surviving members of Nikita's army to the dungeons and locked them up. Alia would deal with them later.

Redka stirred, as his royal faerie blood got to work on his injury. Myanna reported that the dagger had not gone deep enough to cause any real damage. He opened his eyes and stared up into Amber's face.

'Welcome back,' she said.

'Why is it you are always the one to save me, instead of the other way around?'

Amber laughed and kissed him tenderly on the lips. 'If it makes you feel any better, you were on your way to save me when you were hurt. That kind of counts.'

She shrugged her shoulders, and he laughed cupping her face with his hand. 'Thank you,' he said.

He lifted himself up so he could sit with his back to the castle wall. As he looked around at the destruction of the castle, he noticed the figure laid out on the flagstones.

'Aaron?'

Amber shook her head. 'He didn't make it. He sacrificed himself to save you and Myanna.'

Redka clenched his jaw and stared at the fallen warrior. 'He was a good fae, and I never got to tell him.'

'I did. I told him we would always remember him.'

'He will have a full fae service. I will make sure of it.'

Amber smiled and grasped Redka's hand. 'I'm glad you are okay. I don't know what I'd do without you.'

He ran a finger along the scar on her arm where the extraction needle had been inserted. Amber watched him, amazed that the extraction had taken place only a few hours earlier. It seemed like a lifetime had passed.

Connor lowered himself gingerly to sit alongside them, his bandage wound securely round his head and partially covering one eye.

'I'm so sorry Redka. I didn't mean to hurt you.'

'No harm done,' Redka slapped him on the shoulder, 'I'm fine.'

'Alia had foreseen that you'd get hurt, but we all assumed it would be Amber. I can't believe it ended up being me.'

'My mother's visions were not fully formed, because she hadn't restored her full powers. She only saw snap shots or words. When you believe something is going to happen, you can often bring it on yourself. Maybe you should be more like Amber.'

Both Amber and Connor burst out laughing at this.

'He wishes,' Amber teased.

'I reckon I could blow up a rock just as well as you.'

She thumped him on the arm playfully as Redka shook his head in confusion, convinced he would never understand humans.

They were still laughing when Tom burst through the gates with Cass at his side.

Amber leapt to her feet and ran, throwing herself at her best friend.

Tom staggered back as he caught her in his arms, 'Hey cutie, did you miss me?'

'I am so happy to see you,' she cried, 'I missed you, and I was so worried. Then I looked up and you were there, in the sky, riding a dragon!'

'Yeah, Sali is so cool, you have to come and meet her.'

He grabbed her hand and pulled her outside the castle gates to the dusty roadway. The floor was littered with bloody weapons and fallen minotaurs. The road ran red just outside the gateway and Amber swallowed hard to stop herself from vomiting.

'Hold your breath; it helps,' Cass advised as she caught up with them.

The scene was surreal, celebratory on one hand, and a blood bath on the other. The surviving fae folk were jubilant and danced in circles. More of them poured from the treeline as word spread to the surrounding villages.

Tom and Amber walked along the edge of the road that ran parallel to the dried up moat. In the distance she could see a fire burning, and large shadows looming up from the night. She saw Roth standing at the fireside. He looked so much bigger out in the open than he had when he was chained to the cave floor.

'Welcome, little eye,' he boomed across the fire as he saw them approach, 'This must be your Tom.'

Tom placed his hand on his chest and bowed deeply.

'What are you doing?' Amber whispered.

'Roth is the head of the dragon realm. He is like the king, or mayor, or whatever it is, so I'm being polite.'

Amber giggled, 'Since when do you need to impress the head of the dragon realm? Don't tell me, you've fallen in love with his dragon daughter and want to have dragon babies?'

Tom gave her a withering look, 'I see that overthrowing an evil princess and saving a realm hasn't changed you.'

Amber laughed loudly and hugged him again, 'I missed you.'

A large green dragon appeared in front of them, and Tom swept his arm out in a flamboyant gesture, as if he was showing her his latest invention.

'Amber, I would like you to meet Yovan.'

The dragon bobbed his head up and down and then cocked it to the side, 'She's cute, Tom.'

Amber blushed and looked at the ground, while Tom sniggered by her side.

'Yovan is a bit of a lady's dragon,' he told her.

'It's a pity the ladies don't reciprocate though, isn't it, Yovan?' A large red dragon joined them, and bumped into Yovan the same way Amber and Tom slapped each other in their affectionate way.

'I'm Sali,' said the red dragon, 'You must be Amber.'

'Yes, it's a pleasure to meet you both.'

Tom and Yovan returned to the fireside as Sali motioned for Amber to follow her. 'I heard from the faeries that Alia managed to vanquish Nikita. I'm sure that was a tough battle.'

Amber shook her head, 'It was over very fast. Alia threw a couple of golden orbs and Nikita was a pile of ash.'

'Hmm, seems a bit too simple don't you think? Especially after Alia has been missing for so long, and had to cope with all this waiting as she rounded up her followers.'

Amber looked at Sali thoughtfully, 'You don't think it's over?'

'I'm a dragon; we are used to big finishes to our battles with plenty of fire, and this one seemed just to wink out a bit too fast for my liking.'

Amber looked back towards the castle. The sky above glowed orange, yellow and red as the fires still raged. The surrounding area outside was littered with fallen minotaurs and dancing faeries. Her stomach started to churn as she processed Sali's words.

'What are you thinking, little eye?'

'I think you may be right Sali. I'm thinking this is just like the eye of a tornado, and any minute we're all going to get picked up and sucked into hell.'

She started to walk towards the castle, slowly at first, and then breaking into a run as her head pounded.

'I'm right behind you Amber,' Sali called down to her, as she launched herself into the sky. She could hear Tom shouting after her in the distance, but she didn't stop, she couldn't stop. Something was very wrong.

SHE REACHED the dirt track just as a column of black smoke burst through the centre of the roof and shook the foundations of the castle. She stumbled and fell heavily to her knees, throwing her hands out to break her fall. From her position on the ground she could see the inside of the hallway. Black smoke poured from the open gates obscuring her view. She had left her family and friends inside; Myanna, Alan, Redka, Alia, and Connor were all in that hallway.

The ground trembled again, and the faeries on the road stopped their revelry to stare up at the castle.

'Get back,' Amber shouted, 'get to the trees!'

The fae scattered, carrying their injured, and melting into the treeline. Mags rushed up the dirt track to her side, helped her to her feet, and drew his sword.

'What is it?'

Amber looked at him. His face was covered in blood spatters, and his tunic was torn in places where he had been on the receiving end of a spear. He looked tired and swayed on his feet.

'Get to the trees Mags, look after the fae.'

'I won't leave you. Whatever is in there, we can face it together.'

She shook her head, 'No, Mags, we can't. Nikita is too strong.'

Mags gasped and swung to face her, 'Nikita is dead.'

'No, Nikita is alive, but she isn't playing fair.'

She left Mags on the track and ran towards the gates. The tremors were growing stronger, and large chunks of masonry were falling from the walls to crash on the stone floors. The dust billowed around her as she slipped into the castle.

The air was thick with dust and smoke, so she covered her nose and mouth with her hand as she made her way inside. She kept to the side of the hallway, using the wall as a guide as she crept further into the castle.

Her family and friends were nowhere in sight. Aaron's body still lay on the floor where she had left him. Moving silently along the wall, she reached the entrance to the throne room and sneaked a look inside.

Myanna and Alan were suspended in mid-air, alongside Alia and Connor. Their bodies were bound together with dark green tendrils of magic that glowed in the gloom, while their heads were bent as if they were in a deep sleep. She looked around for Redka, but couldn't see him anywhere.

Closing her eyes, she concentrated on her elemental magic and her glamour, feeling for the wisps of smoke that hung in the air and moving them towards the open doors and windows. The air lightened and she had a clear view of the throne room.

A blinding flash of green filled her vision as a magical orb exploded against the doorframe. Amber dived for cover when another orb sailed over her head and crashed into the ceiling. A shower of debris tumbled down over her as she scrambled to the side.

'There is no place to hide, my dear,' Nikita's voice drifted over the groans of the castle walls as they continued to shake.

Amber pulled her power up from the floor and let it flood her system. She could feel the fire race up her legs and along her spine, splintering out along her arms and pooling in the palms of her hands. She glanced down as her fingers turned orange, and tiny flames danced over the surface of her skin. She had been here before and nearly lost herself in the darkness.

'Lavanya, if you can hear me, stay close and keep me safe,' she mumbled under her breath.

She stood up, and calmly walked out into the middle of the doorframe, facing the centre of the room. Nikita stood between her family and friends with her hands in the air and a green orb aimed at both sets of people.

'Any sudden moves and I kill everyone you hold dear.'

'What do you want?'

Nikita laughed. Her black eyes flashed green as she stared at Amber with an intense loathing.

'Isn't it obvious, my dear? I want your powers.'

'That's impossible. First of all, Aaron is dead, so you have nobody to do your extractions. And second of all, I'm not parting with any more of my gifts.'

Her body hummed as she spoke, and the fire churned over and over deep in her stomach. She watched Nikita like a hawk, waiting for the onslaught of dark magic that she knew the evil princess could unleash.

Beyond the broken window, she could hear Sali roar into the night as she circled the castle. The cries of the fae had long since died down, as they all vanished into the safety of the forest. Only the dragons remained, guarding the sky. If Amber failed, then she hoped that Roth, Sali and Yovan could finish the job and free the realm.

Her eyes flitted to Alia briefly, and Nikita chuckled, a deep dark sound that grated on Amber's nerves.

'My sweet sister can't help you now, child. She was foolish to think that her simple light trick could kill me. I am the rightful ruler of this realm, and the powers of the castle are mine.'

She stepped forward slowly and lowered her arms, but kept the orbs trained on their targets. 'Did you know that our father created a spell to bind our royal powers within the golden gates, in case an enemy took the castle? When Alia was taken, the majority of her powers became trapped in the carvings. I tried to extract them, but to no avail, so I turned my talents to extracting powers from other realm leaders.'

Amber had heard the story before. Redka had told her about the carvings on the golden gates, and how his mother's full power was just waiting to be returned. All she needed to do was step foot in the castle and touch the gates. Amber had seen her do this.

'Alia has unlocked her power. Whatever you have done to her won't last, and she's the queen of Avaveil, not you.'

Nikita sneered at her, 'If my sister *had* unlocked her power, then I would have died in that little light show. But as I'm still standing, I can assure you that her powers now belong to me. Our father's spell failed her, left her as a useless creature of the light. Your little friends will only wake up if I allow it.'

The anger began to bubble in Amber's abdomen. Her fingers twitched, and the flames flickered slightly higher. Nikita noticed and raised the green orbs.

'You would be dead before the flames left your hands, little girl.'

Amber lowered her head to the floor. When she raised it she was smiling, a hard smile that held no mirth.

'I'm not a little girl,' she said, 'I'm an oracle.' With that, she launched two great fireballs at Nikita, hitting her in the shoulder and the side. She screamed, and her green orbs withered and disintegrated as she stumbled backwards. Before she could recover, Amber moved on her again. She threw her fire like a whip and curled it around Nikita's body. It snaked around her, curving up her body, and pinning her arms to her sides. Nikita roared and used her dark magic to snap the fiery bindings.

She opened her arms wide and filled the space with a hazy green glow, the stench of death filling the room. Amber staggered backwards.

The dark magic rushed forward, expanding as it moved. Amber threw up her arms, and a white shield blocked its path. Her hands shook with the effort of keeping it steady and holding back the darkness.

Lavanya's voice echoed in her head, *You have the strength, Amber. Do not fear, as we are with you.*

Her body seemed to respond to what she heard, and it filled with a trembling fury and awareness. She was not going to let Nikita win.

She pushed as hard as she could against the white shield, and the darkness exploded in a shower of green sparks.

The fire shot from her palms and caught Nikita in a vice, lifting her off the floor so her feet kicked into the air.

'Free my family, Nikita, and I will spare your life.'

'Oh my dear child, your family are already dead,' she nodded towards where Myanna and Alan hung above the ground, 'They've been dead this whole time.'

A blackness filled Amber's head as she looked over at her parents; her whole body shook as the flames rose higher. The bonds that held Nikita intensified, and she screamed out in pain as the fire burnt into her flesh.

The room began to blur, and Amber could only see her parents. Their lifeless bodies bound together in a loving embrace; their final reunion.

The castle began to buck and twist around them and huge stones fell from the ceiling. The rumble of the dragons in the night sky sounded to Amber like a war cry, and she relished the anger in their anguished roars.

Her hands shook violently as the fire grew, spreading out further and further and igniting anything that stood in its path. Nikita continued to scream and writhe as Amber funnelled more fire at the evil princess.

In the deepest recesses of her mind she could hear Lavanya calling to her, but she closed her mind off to the ancient oracle. Her parents were dead, Alia and Connor were dead, and there was nothing left to make her care.

'Amber, come back to us. All is not lost. Your bond is strong with your prince. Hear him call. Hear him call.'

She blinked against the sting in her eyes, Lavanya's words stirring something within her. Hear him call. Her prince. Redka. Where was Redka?

She snapped her powers back inside herself, and the throne room grew silent. The castle stood very still, and the call of the dragons who guarded the sky ceased to fill the air.

Nikita dropped to the ground as she was released from the fire, the smell of burnt flesh and clothing wafting over to where Amber stood. She gagged and covered her nose and mouth.

Nikita tried to raise her head but she was too weak. Her strength waned and her hands fizzled with a green flicker of dark magic, but it faded quickly. Amber watched as Myanna and Alan's bodies floated to the floor, their legs buckling under them as they dropped. Alia and Connor followed, and sank to the dusty floor with a soft thud.

Amber avoided looking at her family and friends as she towered over her enemy. 'It's over Nikita, you lose. Your powers are too weak for you to fight back.'

Nikita's voice was hoarse when she spoke, a quiet sound that dripped with contempt and hatred. 'I may be weak now, little girl, but I will recover, and I will kill you.'

Amber didn't doubt for a moment that she meant every word she said, and she wondered how she would be able to restrain an evil faerie without Alia's magic.

There was a loud scraping sound from the far corner of the room, and Amber drew a dagger from her belt and held it aloft. The fallen rocks began to shift and fall as someone pushed against them from beneath. Redka emerged from the rubble, covered in dust and small cuts.

Amber watched him appear. Her prince.

He started to run towards her, and she launched herself forward, meeting him halfway. They fell into each other's arms.

'I thought you were dead,' she said, 'There was something wrong, and I came back.'

He kissed her face, covering her cheeks and forehead in small kisses as he held her face between his hands.

'I didn't know where you went. The castle shook and filled with smoke. I ran after you but the wall collapsed, and I couldn't get through.'

She clung to him, resting her head on his shoulder, and coughing as the dust tickled the back of her throat.

'How touching.' Nikita spoke in a low voice. 'The oracle and her prince.'

They both turned towards Nikita. She had managed to lift herself off the floor and was standing in the centre of the room. Her skin smoked where the fire had scorched through her dress.

'How poetic that the two of you will die together.' She raised her hands out to the side and an eerie black smoke emanated from her palms.

Amber felt her fire rush forward and then stop suddenly. She looked down and saw that Redka had laced his fingers through hers. A silver shimmer coated their entwined hands and swept up and over the two of them. They looked into each other's eyes as their powers joined. The oracle power finding the hidden faerie power of the royal bloodline, uniting the two of them for a greater good. They were surrounded by a curtain of silver that rippled like a waterfall.

Before Nikita could unleash her magic, Amber and Redka raised their free hands and fired a silver stream of light. It hit Nikita between the eyes, pushing her head back so far that she faced the ceiling. Together they felt for her magical essence. Like pulling on a piece of string, they tugged at the magical essence that filled Nikita's mind. She screamed as her energy and power unravelled until she was just an empty shell. A powerless fae in a damaged body.

They disconnected from the magic, and Nikita sank to her knees.

'What have you done?' she screamed, holding her head in her hands.

'We have extracted your powers; you have nothing left.'

Amber shook her head as she watched Nikita rocking back and forth, 'How did we do that?'

Redka lifted his hand that still held hers. 'I am a royal fae, and when I entered this castle my mother's powers seeped into me. I hadn't realised this was possible until I felt your pain. I could feel my faerie magic rising and falling, and I could hear Lavanya in my head telling me to get to you.' He smiled down at Amber and gestured towards Nikita. 'She can't harm us now.'

Amber's eyes filled with tears as she looked over at where her parents lay on the floor beside Alia and Connor. 'It's too late; she's already hurt us both more than she knows.' As she said it, there was a small movement in the corner of her eye. She sharpened her gaze and saw it again. Myanna was moving her arm.

'Mum?' Amber ran to her side and knelt on the floor looking at her mother.

Myanna groaned and shifted her head to look up at Amber, 'What happened?'

'Oh mum!' She flung her arms around her and sobbed freely. All around them she could hear movement. First Alan, then Connor, and finally Alia, all began to move.

They all began to hug and talk at the same time as Mags flew into the room with a small group of fae warriors. Tom and Cass appeared at the back and pushed their way to Amber's side.

Alia stood over Nikita and spread her wings, 'Mags, I would like you to secure the prisoner and escort her to the cells. She is to be placed there until I can arrange for her passage to another realm far away from Avaveil.'

Mags nodded and grabbed Nikita's arm, hauling her to her feet, 'It will be a pleasure my queen.'

CHAPTER 15

As the sun rose over the burning remains of the castle, Amber and Redka walked hand in hand along the edge of the dried up moat. Mags and his team were sweeping through the grounds to round up any of Nikita's followers. They were all locked away in the dungeon while Nikita had been placed in Amber's former cell deep in the castle. Redka had placed a binding spell on the small space, but it wasn't necessary. Nikita was no longer a threat. Her powers had been taken away, and she was nothing more than a white-haired human in faerie clothing.

'How did you know that our powers would join?' Amber asked as they walked along the grassy embankment.

'I heard Lavanya in my head and she kept telling me over and over that our bond was strong. When I thought about Connor's dagger striking me, I realised that it should have caused me more harm, but I was fine. My fae powers of healing and strength were growing, but this was something different. Then I remembered my mother talking to me about the spell my grandfather had cast, and that the royal bloodline could release it upon returning to the castle. I just thought it was my mother's rightful power, but as I'm an heir to the throne it found me instead.'

'Nikita is royal blood though, how come it didn't let her use the power?'

'I think her soul had been tainted beyond recognition by the necromancer magic she wielded. The spell of my ancestors just saw her as an enemy.'

They walked in silence for a while, enjoying the warmth of the sun as it lifted higher in the sky. All around them were the sounds of birds chirping and crickets in the grass. The faerie folk had begun to return to the castle and help with the clean-up of the area. It was going to be a very big and long task.

Amber could hear the faint sound of trickling water. She strained to look through the treeline to see if she could spot the source, thinking there must be a waterfall close by. She was about to ask Redka if the Veil River was near to the castle, when she noticed the moat and stopped in her tracks.

The moat surrounded the castle on all sides, with the small dirt track the only access point to the main golden gates. The lord of the woodland village had told her how the moat had dried up after Alia was taken from the realm. 'Our land was in mourning,' he had said.

But now she stood on a green embankment and looked at the clear, clean water lapping gently against the grassy bank. The moat was full once more.

'Did you do that?'

Redka looked sheepishly at the water and shrugged, 'I think the castle knows we've come home.'

The creamy stones gleamed and the water sparkled. Along the bank, tiny wildflowers began to unfurl, facing the bright sunshine.

'It's beautiful,' Amber whispered.

In the distance, they could hear the roar of the dragons as they worked on removing the heavy debris from the castle grounds and rebuilding the walls. Tom and Cass worked with them. They had been inseparable since they had returned to Avaveil. Amber's heart felt heavy at the thought of him having to leave Cass behind. She knew the time was coming when they would return to Hills Heath, but she wasn't ready to think about her sorrow at having to leave

Redka. Only Myanna and Alan would come out of this quest with their hearts intact.

'We should go back and help,' Redka tugged on her hand and they made their way back to the castle.

Mags was carrying Aaron's body out at they approached, and Amber felt a deep sorrow flood through her body.

'Alia is going to hold a full faerie burial for Aaron at the Veil River,' Mags told them, 'I am going to prepare his body.'

Redka bowed his head as Mags passed and squeezed Amber's hand, 'He will have a warrior's funeral.'

She smiled, but it didn't reach her eyes. She couldn't explain to Redka how relieved she felt that it was only Aaron they were burying, and not her entire family. Thinking her parents were dead had almost been the ruin of her. As Lavanya had told her repeatedly, her powers were indeed ruled by her emotions. This was something she wanted to work on when they got home. Myanna was able to teach her about the elemental magic and healing lotions, but unfortunately, her father's powers were gone and lost forever. Or were they?

'Redka, now that Nikita's dark magic has been wiped from the realm, does that mean you would be able to give Ninette and my dad their powers back?'

He thought for a moment, 'I am unsure. Aaron told us that the extraction had been unstable, and Nikita couldn't sustain the powers she received from others, so it may be possible. My mother would know more.'

'Could you try?'

He grinned at her, 'Let's go find Alia and Ninette.'

AS IT turned out, the process was a very simple one. Redka placed his hands over Ninette's head and filled her with his royal fae magic. The results spoke for themselves.

Alia guided Redka as he concentrated on resurrecting Ninette's energies. By passing on his fae magic, this re-awoke a dormant part of the water sprite that closed off when Nikita's necromancers did their evil work. It acted as a safety valve, protecting the host and reserving a small portion of their personal powers. Unfortunately, Patricia had overworked the orc leader, Xavier, leaving him to perish.

A golden aura pulsed around Redka and Ninette as they shared his royal magic. Amber watched in fascination as Ninette's features changed. Her tiny figure began to fill out and smooth over, the dark circles under her eyes vanished, and her skin took on a luminescent glow. Her long, blonde hair looked thicker and bounced around her shoulders. She no longer looked like the frail creature that Amber had met in the cells. She was stunning and powerful, and looking at her now, Amber understood why Nikita had taken her. She was a leader; a strong and beautiful water sprite who commanded attention.

When she opened her eyes, they sparkled a bright blue, dazzling Amber with their intensity. Her smile sent shivers of warmth through Amber's body. Her happiness at being restored was contagious, and they all laughed and cried when Redka disconnected his power.

'Thank you, Prince Redka. I cannot begin to repay you for what you have done for me. I will return to the Great Sea and speak of your courage and power. Should you ever need my assistance, then you only need to call, and I will come.'

Amber hugged her tightly, 'Don't forget to pop in and see me if you're ever in the human world.'

Alia and Redka exchanged a brief look.

'Of course I will, sweet Amber. I am so pleased that the prophecy is true; the last oracle will indeed unite the realms. And if I can help you on your quest, then call my name.'

Amber's brow creased, but she tried not to show her worry. As far as she was concerned her quest was over. She had travelled to Phelan and saved her friend. That in turn brought about a chain of events that she had no control over. It was done. The good guys had won and her quest was complete. Tom was safe, she and Connor had survived, and the bonus of reuniting Myanna and Alan was the cherry on top. But it was time to go home. It was time to be with her parents and return to being a normal girl.

Ninette walked away with Alia as they discussed her return to the Great Sea.

'What was all that about?' Amber asked Redka when Ninette and Alia had left the room.

Redka shrugged as he set about lifting the oak table from its side and returning it to the centre of the room. The two of them dragged the chairs from the rubble as they spoke.

'Mags is escorting Ninette down the Veil River to the gateway to the Great Sea. He is transporting the minotaurs. Apparently the gateway to the Ruined Lands is on the way, and they can deliver Nikita's broken army back to their home realm for punishment. Alia has asked Ninette to seal their gateway, so they can never return to Avaveil.'

'No, not that,' she shook her head, 'I mean the oracle quest. Everyone keeps going on about my destiny and the prophecy, but I'm finished. I just want to go home.'

Redka stopped moving furniture and looked at her from across the room. A heavy weight descended over her as she looked at the pain in his eyes.

'Does it mean anything to you that I want you to stay here with me?'

'Of course it does,' she spoke softly, 'This is the hardest decision I've ever had to make, Redka. I love you so much, but I don't belong in your world. I have a home and a family.'

'I can be your family.'

She smiled at him, 'You are my family, you will always be here,' she placed a hand over her heart, 'but I can't stay.'

Connor burst into the room carrying a mound of pale green fabric. He stopped abruptly in the doorway, realising he was interrupting something important.

'Sorry, I just wanted to tell you we are ready for Aaron's ceremony. Alia sent you both a robe to wear.'

He dropped the clothes on the table and left.

Redka and Amber hadn't moved. They remained looking at each other across the room for a long while. Eventually, Redka reached for a robe and slipped it over his head.

THE VEIL River was a vast expanse of water that stretched off far into the distance. Along its banks were small villages that used the waterway to trade with the larger towns within the realm. The fall of the castle had affected trade heavily, and many of the villages had struggled to feed themselves over the years.

Amber looked along the riverbank at the fae folk who lined both sides. They were thin and pale, with tattered tunics, but their faces shone with renewed hope. The female fae flittered across the river, their strong wings glistening in the midday sun, as they dropped flower petals over the water.

The boats that would transport Ninette, Mags, and the prisoners to the gateway for the Great Sea and the Ruined Lands sat in wait at the point where the river forked in two. The two smaller sections wound through the heart of Avaveil like veins. The left-hand stream flowed close to the woodland village, where the lord and his villagers could be seen standing in a uniformed line. The lord wore his light green funeral robe, and dabbed at his eyes with a small handkerchief. He, like Amber, had taken a while to trust Aaron, but now understood just how much he had sacrificed to help the realm.

Alia and Redka stood at the front of the crowd, close to the water's edge. Aaron's body had been bound in a beautiful green silk sheet that was edged in gold. Flowers surrounded him as he lay in the middle of a wooden raft that was tethered to a small jetty.

'We send our loyal warrior to the afterlife.' Alia's clear voice carried over the water to reach all who had gathered to show their respects. 'He will join our great and wise ancestors so he can learn the lessons of reincarnation, to return to us in another form and another lifetime.'

Redka set the raft loose and dropped a flaming torch onto the wood as it drifted peacefully out into the river. As the current caught it, the flames grew, and Aaron's body was engulfed in the fire. The faeries who lined the river bank tossed flowers out onto the water as the raft floated past. A tear escaped and trailed down Amber's cheek as she watched the fire rage.

'Rest in peace, Aaron,' she whispered, 'and thank you.'

With the ceremony over, the fae folk began to disperse, returning to their villages or to help with the restoration of the castle. Alia greeted many of them as they walked, hugging children and shaking hands with their lords. It was clear on everyone's faces that all loved Alia. Amber felt a sense of peace when she watched Alia talking to her people. She felt pride at being able to help make this possible.

Tom bounded up next to her and threw his arm over her shoulder, 'Hey cutie, how are you holding up?'

'I'm doing okay. It was sad to say goodbye to Aaron, but it also felt like he was with us, if you know what I mean.'

Tom nodded, 'Cass said that the fae believe they reincarnate as something else, so he might already be one of those birds in the sky or a rabbit in the meadow.'

She smiled at that; it was a lovely thought.

He dropped his arm and kept pace with her as they followed the stream back towards the castle.

'I need to tell you something,' he said, 'and you're not going to like it.'

She looked up at him and noticed the creases around his eyes as he screwed his face up. He used to do that just before he had to tell her that he'd broken her ruler or lost her textbook.'

'What have you done this time?' she asked in the mock teacher voice that used to make them laugh.

'I'm staying.' He said it so quietly she almost missed it.

She stopped walking suddenly, and a small group of faeries had to swerve to miss crashing into the back of her.

'What do you mean you're staying?'

'I'm staying behind, with Cass.' He gave her his trademark lopsided smile, but she couldn't find the strength to think it was endearing.

'You can't. We belong in Hills Heath, not here.' Her head was full of noise and snippets of conversations. Pictures of the two of them rolled around her mind. When they were seven and built a book fort, when they climbed the neighbour's tree to steal an apple, all the times they had snuggled on Amber's bed and vented about his parents and her father.

'You above all people know that I never felt like I belonged back home. When I was in the dragon realm, with Cass and her family, it felt so right. I knew I'd come home. Cass makes me happy, and the dragons, well they're just so cool. I know this is hard for you to understand. You've got what you want, your family is back together, but for me, what I want is here, and so I'm staying.'

She couldn't find the words. He looked so grown up and strong, not the boy next door that had been her best friend forever. He was a man now.

She wrapped her arms around his neck and hugged him, 'I will support you in whatever you decide. If you need to stay, then that's okay. I will always be here for you. I'm not sure what the mobile reception is like in these parts, but I'm only a gateway away.'

He chuckled in her ear and squeezed her tightly, 'Thank you, Amber. That means so much to me. We are planning on leaving tonight with the dragons, so knowing you're not mad at me makes it a little bit easier.'

She pressed her eyes closed and tried not to cry. Tonight was only a few hours away, hardly any time left at all. She could think of a million things she wanted to say, but couldn't find the voice to say them. Instead, she kissed his cheek and ran off towards the trees.

CASS FOUND her an hour later outside the willow tree house that Redka had built for them. She lay on the ground staring up at the clouds as they floated past.

'Hi, do you mind if I join you?' Cass asked.

Amber lifted her head to look at her and then patted the grass beside her. Cass sat down and hugged her knees to her chest.

'I hope you can forgive me, Amber.'

'Why do I need to forgive you?'

'For taking Tom away. I know how close the two of you are.'

She took a deep breath, and pushed from her mind images of them riding their bikes and kicking up the leaves on their walk to school.

'Tom knows his mind, Cass, and he loves you. It's only right that he gets to do what makes him happy.'

'So you are not mad?'

'Of course not. If anything, I'm jealous.'

Cass looked down at Amber, 'Why?'

'I'm not jealous of you Cass; I don't mean it in that way. The two of you are perfect for each other. I'm jealous that he has been able to follow his heart. I have to leave to take my parents home and return Connor to his aunt. They...we belong in the human realm. My father has been through so much and needs to have some peace in his life. Myanna needs time to remember how great we were as a family. But...'

She stopped talking and sat up. Cass didn't push her. She just waited patiently for Amber to get the jumble of thoughts in her head straight.

'I love Redka and I don't want to leave him. So you see, Tom has followed his heart, and I have to follow my head, and that makes me jealous.'

'I'm sure you will find a way, Amber. If he is worth it, then you have to find a way.'

They sat in silence listening to the sounds of the forest, as Amber tried desperately to detach herself from the huge battle between her head and heart that raged inside her.

CHAPTER 16

Roth nudged Amber's shoulder with his snout and huffed, causing her hair to ruffle.

'I'm going to miss you, little eye,' he said.

Amber ran her hand up the side of his face, his leathery, white skin felt dry and hard to the touch. His cuts had begun to heal, and Myanna's lotions had made sure that the deeper lacerations would not become infected.

'Look after Tom for me,' she said, 'He likes to get himself in trouble occasionally.'

Roth chuckled and nodded his huge head, 'I will watch him closely.'

Sali approached and lowered her head down to Amber, 'You are a brave and proud young woman, and it has been an honour to fight alongside you.'

'Likewise, Sali, and thank you for guiding me.'

'You don't need much guiding, little eye, your talents are impressive. In fact, I think you would make a wonderful dragon.'

They laughed, and Amber hugged Sali's immense head.

Tom appeared at her shoulder and gave her a small smile, 'It's time to go.'

Sali gave them some privacy as she barked orders at the younger dragons and dragged Yovan away from the crowd of female faeries he had attracted.

'I'm going to miss you so much.' She fidgeted on the spot.

'You'll always be my best friend, cutie, even if you learn to levitate or turn invisible with those oracle powers of yours. To me, you'll always be my Amber.'

She laughed through the veil of tears that streamed down her face, 'Just for the record I've done the levitating part, but if I manage the rest I'll let you know.'

'Cool!' he said as he gathered her up in his arms. 'Stay safe and follow your heart, cutie.'

She blinked at him as he stepped back. Cass had climbed up onto Yovan's back, and Sali was hovering waiting for Tom. He saluted at Redka and Connor, who stood a short distance away and hopped up onto Sali's back.

'Mr. and Mrs. N, it's been great catching up. Hope to see you again. Your Majesty, I am forever in your service.' He bowed his head at Alia, who smiled affectionately up at him.

Finally, he looked at Amber, 'I love you,' he mouthed, as Sali lifted up from the floor and flapped her massive wings. They soared into the sky and circled over the group before moving off into the distance and the great cloud gateway.

Amber stayed put until she could no longer see the dragons. She watched the spot in the sky with a heavy heart, convinced that if she moved she would break apart.

Myanna wrapped her arm around Amber's shoulder.

'He's a good lad Amber, he'll be fine.'

'I know,' she whispered, afraid that if she spoke any louder her voice would crack.

'Come on, let's go get something to eat.'

They wandered slowly back up to the castle. It was strange to see the elemental magic beginning to seep back into the land. The grass looked greener, the sky bluer. The dusty track that led up to the gates and over the moat had been swept clear, revealing a patchwork of coloured stones beneath. The bustle of the castle could be heard from the road. Faerie warriors worked on clearing the rubble, while Alia bestowed her magic within the walls. She taught Redka how to manipulate the air to remove the dust, and how to brighten the darkest corner with the golden light of their royal bloodline.

It was a delight to see, and despite the aching hole in Amber's heart where her friend had been, she couldn't help but marvel at the resilience of the realm.

THEY HAD a huge feast that night with all the surrounding villagers as guests of honour. There was music and dancing, and the atmosphere was electric.

Amber didn't stay for long. The tears she had shed that day had left her feeling sleepy. She wished everyone a good night and slipped out of the throne room before Redka could see her. He was seated at his mother's side, the rightful place for an heir to the throne. She was happy that he would have a greater purpose once she left. It would keep him busy and he wouldn't need to give her a second thought.

She opened the door to her room; a small stone chamber with a large wooden bed. The covers were a deep, shimmering purple. Piles of scatter cushions were illuminated in the moonlight that streamed through the window. She changed into a clean tunic and slid between the covers. There was a soft tapping sound at her door and she flopped back on her bed, too tired to lift her weary limbs to answer.

'It's open,' she called.

The door creaked open and Redka stepped into the room. The hole in her heart opened up even wider at the sight of him, and she swallowed down the overwhelming urge to burst into tears.

'You left without saying goodnight,' he said.

'I didn't want to disturb you. It looked like you were having fun being a Prince.' She smiled at him as he closed the door and walked over to sit on the bed.

'I was. There are so many people who need help, and for once I will be able to do some good.'

'You've always been able to do that, Redka. Whatever you say or do can brighten someone's day.'

He leant down and pressed his lips to hers and she responded by kissing him back. She could feel the roller coaster whirling in the pit of her stomach, as his kisses deepened. He ran his fingers lightly along her arm, and she shivered.

'Will you stay with me tonight?' she asked, suddenly feeling very shy. 'Just hold me while I sleep?'

He cupped her face and kissed her nose tenderly. Kicking off his boots, he swung his legs up onto the bed and settled alongside Amber on top of the covers. She rested her head on his chest and listened to his heart beating as she drifted off to sleep.

THE BROKEN *window of the throne room filled with a dark cloud and a pulsing smoke swirled through the open space and filled the room. Amber could see her family and friends dancing in the middle of the floor; the villagers surrounded them as they laughed and sang.*

She wanted to warn them, but her limbs wouldn't move. She tried to shout, but her voice was drowned out by the noise of the music.

No one could see the black tendrils as they invaded the castle. They swept over the ceiling and snaked along the walls until the entire room was gloomy. Yet the party still went on; everyone was oblivious to the changes in their environment.

Amber could see her mother and father in the centre of the floor. They were holding each other up, and swaying together in a lover's dance that nobody else was a part of.

Like a spotlight shining on them from above, the black clouds parted to reveal only them. They looked so happy, and Amber trembled as she watched them. Something was coming.

She cried out for them to move, to notice what was going on. They both looked up at the same time and stared straight at her. She shouted at them but they didn't move. They smiled and gave her a wave, as she struggled against the invisible ties that held her back.

A figure stepped out of the blackness—a creature so grotesque that Amber gagged. Its skin hung in sheets from its wizened frame, and its matted hair sat in charred clumps atop its head.

Swivelling its scrawny neck, the creature looked at Amber and grinned.

The eyes that stared back at her were unmistakeable, and Amber screamed.

IT HAD been a long while since Amber's last vision, and she had hoped that with her journey to Phelan and subsequent quest that the visions were gone for good.

Redka had soothed her when she awoke in a panic screaming, and managed to guide her back to sleep, but she felt jumpy and out of sorts.

The morning didn't bring any sense of comfort for her either, and she wandered around the corridors and rooms of the castle in a foggy daze.

On the bright side, she was beginning to see the signs of how Avaveil had once looked before General Loso took Alia, leaving Nikita to plunder and burn the realm.

The main road past the castle was full of brightly coloured market stalls, and the people of Avaveil were tentatively stepping back into their long forgotten routines.

Amber left the castle and wandered along the main street. The stalls were packed with fruit and cheese, breads and cakes. There were woollen shawls, handcrafted shoes in a range of colours, and the smell of herbs, lotions, jams, and broth filled the air.

She came to a small stall where an old rosy-faced faerie sat carving figurines from tree branches.

'When the branches fall, I collect them and give them a new purpose,' she told Amber, who marvelled at the tiny figures and animal carvings on the table.

Her eyes were drawn to a carved dragon with a warrior on its back. She smiled as she thought of Tom, off on his adventure.

'Take it,' said the old faerie, pressing the figurine into Amber's palm, 'as a gift.'

Amber tried to protest, but the old fae was adamant. 'They will always be with you in your heart but this may bring you some comfort on a lonely day.'

Amber smiled and thanked the woman, who carried on with her carving while humming a tune. She wondered how much this old faerie had seen in her many years.

She carried on walking until she reached the entrance to the castle. Connor stood at the end of the walkway with his arms crossed over his chest.

'Been shopping?' he said, nodding at her carved figurine.

'It was a gift.'

'He'll be okay you know.'

'Yeah, I know, I just miss him. We've been through so much, not just in Phelan and here, but throughout our lives. He was always there when I needed him, and I was there for him.' She stroked the figurine, 'We still have each other though, don't we Connor? Once we get home, I'm sure India will have plenty for us to do.'

Connor didn't answer, and Amber started to repeat herself, thinking he hadn't heard, when he interrupted her.

'I'm not going home, Amber. I'm staying behind too.'

She felt like she had been winded in the stomach with a large bat. Connor's head hung low as he kicked at a stone on the ground. She could feel the hole in her heart constrict with every passing second. Was she really about to lose all her friends in the space of twenty-four hours?

'I don't know what to say.' It was the truth. She was speechless. 'What about India? I'm sure your aunt will want you to come home.'

He shook his head, 'I've spoken to her, she understands. Alia gave me a crystal, and between us we managed to hook up a way to communicate between the realms. That's good news. It means we can still stay in touch.' He tried to sound eager, but he knew he was offering her a lame replacement.

'If it's what you want, then I'm happy for you Connor. As I said to Tom, it's important to follow your heart.'

'Is that what you're doing?'

She laughed sarcastically, 'My heart imploded some time ago, so I can only follow my head now. I have the chance to start over with my family, so there's no other choice.'

'There's always a choice Amber. Have you spoken to Myanna, or to your dad? Maybe they want to stay too?'

'It's funny because when I first found my mother, she was adamant that when we got to Avaveil she would be staying with Alia. It hurt like hell when I thought we could be separated again. But then she and my dad were reunited, and they discovered how strong their love was. Nothing will keep them apart anymore. They are ready to live a quiet life, and I can't be the one to take that away from them.'

'They have each other. Who do you have?'

Amber flinched as if she had just been slapped hard. Connor watched her reaction but didn't move. His eyes said it all. She was leaving her first love behind, along with her friends, so that she could chase the dream of a lost childhood.

'I need to go pack.' She stormed off into the castle without looking back.

THE THRONE room looked totally different as Amber walked through the doorway. The stone throne had been removed, and replaced with a large seating area with cushions and throws. A low table sat to the side, filled with a vase of flowers and a bowl of fresh fruit. The window had been replaced much to Amber's delight. Her vision of the evil black smoke seeping through the broken glass resurfaced briefly. She shoved the image deep into the recesses of her mind and painted on a false smile.

The large oak table now sat in a place of pride, with a huge candelabra in the centre. Platters of ham, cheese, bread, and fruit covered the surface as the assembled guests milled around chatting and eating. This was Alia's way to say goodbye, to throw a lavish party and pretend that everybody was fine, and the pain wasn't suffocating them.

Redka handed her a goblet filled with oddly coloured liquid.

'It's a delicacy,' he said, 'made from the sap of the oak trees.'

She scrunched up her nose and set the goblet down on the nearest table. She wasn't in the mood to eat or drink.

'Connor tells me he is staying in Avaveil.'

'Yes,' she said softly, trying to avoid looking into his big purple eyes.

'Are you okay about this?'

'No, but then I'm not okay about any of it.' She felt her fingers begin to tingle and her feet vibrate, and Redka took a step back. 'I don't want to leave either, Redka. I love you, and I desperately want to stay here, but I'm so torn between you and my family.' Her voice was getting louder the more animated she got. She waved her hands about as she talked, trying to shake off the tremors.

'Tell me what to do. Please, Redka, help me.' She pleaded with him, and he pulled her into the circle of his arms.

'I can't tell you what to do, Amber, the decision has to be yours, but just look at your parents. They are so happy that, if you did decide to stay, I'm sure they would be fine.'

Amber looked over at her parents. She could see her mother and father in the centre of the floor. They were holding each other up and swaying together in a lover's dance that nobody else was a part of.

A cold chill spread over her as she watched them. She had seen this before; this entire scene was playing out exactly as it had in her vision. The sound of people singing and laughing echoed off the stone walls as her friends new and old chatted and danced.

'Redka, something's wrong,' she spoke with an urgency in her voice that frightened her. She knew that the evil was approaching, but she didn't know where it was coming from. Looking at the far wall, she could see the huge window looking out over the forest. The glass was intact, and the flickering candlelight bounced off its surface.

'What's wrong?' Redka had picked up on her rising panic and matched it. He could feel her power flowing into her palms and he could taste the fear in her aura, 'Amber, tell me what is happening.'

'It's Patricia,' she said, scanning the room for any dark shadows.

'Patricia is dead, she fell from the window, and Alan saw her fall.'

'He saw her fall, but he didn't see her land. She is one of the most powerful necromancers alive, don't you think she would be able to save herself from such a fate?'

'If that's true then I must alert Alia, she can put extra guards on watch...'

His voice was drowned out as the huge glass window exploded. The shards of glass hurtled into the room, showering the guests with a million daggers. Many of the assembled fae fell to the ground, with pieces of the window embedded in their head, chest and arms.

Screams ricocheted off the walls as people scattered in all directions. The scene was one of chaos. The villagers jostled towards the doorway, pushing over one another to reach the safety of the hallway.

Amber looked over the fleeing heads to see if she could find Patricia in the gaping hole left in the glass. Alia and Connor were herding people out of the room, grabbing the children from the floor and rushing them out into the corridors.

Redka laced his fingers through Amber's hand, 'Stronger together, remember.'

She pushed forward towards the centre of the room where she had last seen her parents. They were gone, swept along in the panicked rush. She craned her neck to see over the swarm of people.

'Where are my parents?'

Redka looked around, searching the faces for Myanna and Alan. Connor arrived at their side and tried to drag them out of the throne room. Amber stood her ground.

'No, Connor, this is my fight.' She pulled her arm from his grasp and waded into the crowd with Redka still holding on tightly to her hand.

At the far side of the room, Amber spotted the long snaking fingers of the black smoke beginning to creep into the building. She had to find her parents before the darkness came.

'Mum! Dad!' She screamed at the top of her lungs, searching frantically. Suddenly, she spotted Myanna's head over by the broken window.

'Mum!' She pulled Redka after her and darted around the last of the guests who was injured and disoriented.

A large slice of glass was protruding from Myanna's stomach when they reached her. She was gripping the shard between her hands and ripping her palms to shreds. Blood poured over her dress and soaked her legs. Redka took charge and moved Myanna to the side of the room where he carefully extracted the glass and began healing the wound. Myanna's face grew paler as her eyes fluttered shut, but Redka didn't stop.

Amber dropped to the floor next to her father who had been hit in the leg by another larger fragment.

'Redka is just helping mum and then we can sort you out.'

Alan nodded and squeezed her hand, 'Don't worry, I've been through worse sweetheart.'

The sound of thunder rumbled through the room as the black clouds swirled thicker and faster. Amber stood in front of the window and channelled her protective energy. If Patricia was about to show herself, then Amber was going to be ready.

Right on cue, the necromancer stepped through the black cloud into the room. The smell of rotting flesh wafted over Amber, and she gagged.

'Don't come any closer, bitch.' Amber faced her, two orbs of fire raised and ready.

The thing that was Patricia laughed a rasping sound like fingernails on a chalkboard.

'You are no match for me,' she hissed, 'You think your oracle powers can stop me? Nikita thought she could harm me, but she had no idea of the power I can conjure.'

The blackness crept along the walls on either side of Amber. She could see the tendrils working their way into the castle from the corner of her eye.

Redka and Myanna were frozen to the spot as the black cloud coated them. Amber's eyes flicked to Redka, who could only blink, his limbs solid, snared in the necromancer's trap.

'Leave my friends alone, Patricia. If it's me you want, then let's sort this out together, girl to girl.' She watched the necromancer shift forward slowly and raised her fiery orbs, 'Or should I say girl to the evil creature?'

'You always were so insolent, never a kind word to say. It will be a relief to be rid of you brat.'

Another step forward and Amber was ready to throw the orbs, but Patricia halted and looked around the room until finally settling her evil glare on Alan, who lay on the floor. The large piece of glass sticking out of his leg was covered in blood as it pooled beneath him.

'My poor love, you're hurt,' she shifted her feet.

'Don't move another muscle, Patricia, or I will kill you.'

'How cruel you are. Your father is lying here injured, and you won't help him. So typical of your generation, only thinking of yourself and never of others. How many years did you make him suffer from your hurtful comments and missing your curfew, you vile child.'

'I'm not the vile thing in this room, Patsy. We both know what you did, so your rantings and false bravado won't work anymore. Leave us alone and slither back to where you came from.'

She glared at Amber with dark black eyes. Amber could feel her watching the orbs of fire dancing in her upturned palms and calculating her chances.

'You're not going to win this Patricia, so just leave us alone.'

The blackness swirled around her, swelling until it blotted out the broken window just behind her. Within the clouds, Amber could make out shapes emerging, a scene unfolding within the twists and turns of the smoke.

A huge building rose up out of the smog with sharp points and an iron drawbridge. It was a dark grey colour, with a slate roof and slits for windows. All around the perimeter were swamp lands, a huge cesspool of bubbling liquid hidden amongst the blood red reeds.

Screams carried on the sooty wind that blasted the sides of the building. Amber shivered involuntarily.

'Don't you like my home?' asked Patricia as she watched for Amber's reaction, 'This is where you want me to slither back to.'

'It's the kind of place I would expect you to come from, black and grey and evil to the very core.'

'Home is not about the place or the building; home is where our loved ones live. I'm sure even this place would feel like home soon enough.'

Amber's eyes flicked between the gruesome image in the smoke and Patricia.

'If you think you're taking me to that place then you're mistaken. My home is here with my family.'

'That's what I thought you might say.'

Before Amber could react, Patricia slithered forward and grabbed Alan round the throat. She reached down and pulled the glass from his leg, tossing the shard to the floor with a clatter.

Alan screamed and clutched his leg.

'Dad!' Amber stepped forward, holding the orbs up higher. However, she didn't have a clean shot at the necromancer. She manhandled Alan to a standing position and skulked behind him, using him as a human shield.

Her charred hands wrapped around his throat as she backed up towards the broken window.

'Let him go and you can live,' Amber shouted, the desperation clear in her voice.

'I have no intention of letting him go child. Alan belongs to me. Home is where your loved ones live, and we have lived together for so long that it's impossible to be apart. Surely you recognise this feeling. You and your prince are bound together. Living apart would kill you both.'

Amber began to feel the panic rise up in her throat. Patricia was dangerously close to the edge of the window and the sheer drop. If she jumped and took Alan with her, he probably wouldn't survive the fall. Her hands throbbed with the elemental magic that flooded her system. In sheer temper she threw a fireball at the ceiling above Patricia's head and the crash echoed around them as Patricia cackled.

'What a shame, all that power and you can't use it for fear of hurting your daddy. What a waste. I'm sure your ancient oracles will be wishing they had a different descendant than a stroppy school girl with an attitude.'

An idea sparked in Amber's head and she concentrated on her glamour gift and channelled the black clouds that swarmed all around them. They left a metallic taste on her tongue as she connected with them. If she timed it just right, she could launch herself at Patricia, grabbing Alan as she did, and knocking them all through the window. Using her glamour, she and Alan could float easily to the ground.

She raised more of her fire from the ground and took a step forward.

'This is your last chance Patricia, let my father go, or I will kill you.'

Patricia tightened the hold on Alan's throat, and he gasped for breath. This was the last straw for Amber. She threw herself forward, tossing the fire behind them to light up the sky and illuminate the image that wavered in the clouds.

Patricia was ready for her and pushed herself backwards, dragging Alan with her. They started to fall as Amber jumped clear of the broken window. Her fingertips brushed her father's arm briefly, but then he was gone. Alan and Patricia were sucked into the cloud with the sharp building and the iron drawbridge.

'No!' She had almost reached him. Her fingers grazed his skin, but it wasn't enough. Patricia had won after all.

The clouds dissipated and crumbled, and she could hear Redka shout out after her as she fell through the gap.

Her connection to the black clouds vanished as they were sucked into Patricia's portal. Amber fell as the air rushed past her and the ground approached at great speed. She had closed her eyes before she hit the floor of the courtyard, holding the image of her father in her mind.

SHE WOKE up to hushed voices, but couldn't make out the words. Her head pounded, her bones ached, and the smell of herbal potions invaded her nostrils. She coughed, but regretted it immediately as a sharp pain shot through her.

'Amber?' Myanna leaned over her, and checked her forehead with the back of her hand. 'How do you feel?'

'Like I fell out of a window.'

Myanna sat back on the bed with a thump and a short laugh, 'Thank goodness. I didn't know if I could heal you. We've tried everything, but with your healing powers gone it was so difficult.'

Connor appeared in her line of sight and smiled down at her, 'You look like hell.'

She rolled her eyes, 'Thanks.'

'Amber, can you remember what happened?' Myanna held her hand and began patting it in an annoyingly affectionate way.

'Patricia took dad and I was too slow to save him.'

'You were incredibly brave. None of us could have known that she had the power to open a portal. The gateways have been the only way to travel between the realms for thousands of years. Portals can only be used within a realm, never to jump between them. She has a lot of power, and you're lucky to have survived at all.'

'I touched him. I had my fingertips on him when he vanished. If I'd been faster, then I could have prevented it and saved him.'

'I could never have forgiven myself if I'd lost you both,' Myanna said.

Amber tried to lift herself up, but cried out as the pain crippled her body.

'Don't move, please, Amber. You've broken a lot of bones, and I'm worried you have internal bleeding. We've worked so hard to keep you stable, and Redka has hardly left your side.'

'Where is he?'

'I'm here, Amber,' his voice carried over to her as he stepped into the room, 'I went to get more herbs from the store. I wasn't expecting you to wake up yet.'

'How long have I been out?'

'Three days,' Connor said before Myanna could stop him. She looked at him and shook her head.

Amber tried to move again, 'That's too long. I have to save my dad.

Redka gently pressed her shoulders back against the bed and smoothed her hair, 'All in good time, Amber. We have sent warriors to speak with all the gateways to see if they have seen Patricia or Alan. We will find him, and we will save him.'

'I know where they are,' she said, 'I saw the place where she took him. It was awful, and he won't survive for long. Please, Redka, help me.'

'What can I do?'

'Give me back my powers. You did it for Ninette, it might work on me too. I could heal myself, and we could set off to save my dad before the week is out.'

Myanna jumped off the bed, 'Even if it worked and you got your healing powers back, do you honestly think it's a good idea to chase across the realms searching for them? You could get yourself killed.'

'Mum, you of all people should understand why I have to do this. Our family has just been reunited, and that evil bitch has managed to rip us apart once again. She has to pay.'

Alia walked into the room and stopped at the end of the bed. 'Amber has a point,' she said. 'I have heard word from our friends in the forest realm that rumours are stirring in the Lost Lands. The necromancers have found themselves a leader and appear to be preparing for war against the other realms. What worries me the most is that they don't want to conquer the other realms, but they want to kill every living thing in them.

'So Patricia is working for yet another power crazy boss and you're expecting Amber to do something about it?' It was Connor who spoke this time, voicing the anxiety that hung on everyone's lips.

Alia shook her head, 'No, Connor, I am not expecting Amber to do this. Not on her own, at least.'

'But you do expect her to do something?'

'It is written in the prophecy; the last oracle will unite the realms. I'm sorry, Connor, but Amber's fate is already mapped out for her. It is our role to help her along the way. But I do have to ask her one question.'

'What's that?'

Alia turned back to Amber, 'Are you ready to accept your destiny and travel across the realms, uniting us as allies against the darkest evil that any of us has ever faced?'

Amber looked at the sea of faces around her bed. Redka's huge purple eyes were full of love and protection. Connor's flashed between his human brown and fae purple, as he tried to come to terms with what was coming. Myanna just looked tired. She smiled weakly, and Amber reached for her hand, squeezing it as tightly as she could manage without causing herself too much pain.

She levelled her gaze on Alia.

'I accept.'

DEAR READER

I hope you enjoyed reading *Guardians of the Sky* as much as I enjoyed writing it. Amber, Connor and Redka have been a huge part of my life over the past few years and I'm so excited about their story. In book three there are a few surprise twists that were instigated by the characters—I'm just the writer, these guys drive the story!

There are a few ways that you, as the avid reader, can get involved in the story too. It would mean the world to me if you could leave an honest review of my book on Amazon or Goodreads. Reviews are important for independent authors and it helps to spread the word.

I also love to interact with readers on my social media pages:

Facebook: *FantasyAuthorSLWilson*

Twitter: *ShelleyWilson72*.

If you're on Instagram then why not share a photo of you with your copy of *Guardians of the Sky* and tag me in *authorslwilson*.

All that's left to say is a huge thank you for joining me, Amber, Connor and Redka on this adventure and I hope you join us for the grand finale in book three. It's going to be an explosive ride!

Hugs and faerie kisses
Shelley x

COMING DECEMBER 2016

BOOK THREE OF THE GUARDIANS

GUARDIANS
OF THE
LOST LANDS

BY
S.L. WILSON

BE PART OF THE ADVENTURE
Sign up to receive
up-to-date news, release dates,
cover reveals, and competitions
before anyone else.

www.shelleywilsonauthor.co.uk

Acknowledgments

In no particular order, I'd like to thank:

My three amazing children, your endless encouragement has been my lifeline. Your unwavering belief that I would succeed kept me writing. I love you so much xxx

My incredible parents who have celebrated every high point and been there to dust me down when I hit a low point. You encouraged me at every stage and supported me through life. I love you both and continue to be inspired by your actions xx

My family and friends. You have listened to my stories and given me feedback; you became the voice of encouragement when I needed it. You are my inspiration x

Thank you to Rick, for his patience, professionalism and dedication to helping me bring this book to life, and to Fiona, for her assistance with a red pen.

The list would not be complete without a shout out for Blue Harvest Creative. You guys keep me sane, keep me writing, and keep me laughing. Thank you from the bottom of my heart.

Finally, thank you to you, the reader, for picking up this book in the hope you will be entertained. I hope I lived up to your expectations.

Thank you all.

About the Author

Shelley Wilson divides her writing time between her young adult fantasy novels, and the motivational non-fiction titles she writes for adults.

Her fantasy series combine myth, legend and faerie tales with a side order of demonic chaos. Inspired by Enid Blyton and the Faraway Tree, Shelley began weaving tales around witches, dragons and faeries from a young age.

Shelley lives in the West Midlands, UK with her three teenage children and an enormous goldfish. She is at her happiest with a slice of pizza, a latte and *Game of Thrones* on the TV. She would love to live in the Shire but fears her five foot ten inch height may cause problems. She is an obsessive list writer, social media addict and full-time daydreamer.

Made in the USA
Charleston, SC
25 January 2016